TALES OF MAGIC CITY

**Also by
Joe Cron:**

Novels
Eve of Demons
The Holitaph
Alden Bridge

Short Stories
The Magistrate
Hellish
Goose
Fate
Jacob's Justice
Granted
The White Dress
A Rare Bird
Henry and Beth at the Funeral Home
The Earthbloods of Carapet
The Untimely Demise of Rachel Tamson
Let the Families Be Joined
Art of the Homeless
Morning Sun

Tales
of
Magic
City

Joe Cron

LARDIN PRESS

Copyright Information

Tales of Magic City
© 2025 by Joe Cron
Published 2025 by Lardin Press
www.lardinpress.com
Cover art copyright © 2023 by Joe Cron
Book and cover design copyright © 2023 by Joe Cron
Cover design by Joe Cron, Lardin Press

ISBN-13: 978-1-949047-03-5
ISBN 10: 1-949047-03-5

"Case Cracked" by Joe Cron was first published in *Fiction River: Fantastic Detectives*, edited by Kristine Kathryn Rusch, WMG Publishing, 2014.

"Caribou Road" by Joe Cron was first published in *Joyous Christmas – A Holiday Anthology*, edited by Kristine Kathryn Rusch, WMG Publishing, 2020, but first published as part of the WMG Holiday Spectacular 2019 project.

"The Murders in the Room Org" by Joe Cron is published for the first time in this volume.

"Morning Sun" by Joe Cron was first published online by *White Cat Publications*, May 2023.

"The White Dress" by Joe Cron was first published by Lardin Press, May 2012.

Contents

Introduction

Welcome! I am absolutely thrilled to bring this volume of stories to life. One of my very favorite characters to write is the intrepid egg detective Frank Dumpty, and this collection debuts my first Frank Dumpty novelette, "The Murders in the Room Org." The first two stories here, the short stories "Case Cracked" and "Caribou Road," were both released previously by WMG Publishing, but this is the first release of either from my imprint, Lardin Press, and it is very exciting! I certainly hope you enjoy these, and thanks!

—Joe Cron
White Lake, Michigan
July 29, 2025

Case Cracked

Joe Cron

The pavement gleamed with the oily sheen of avarice. Streetlights fashioned a weary column down the block, struggling in their losing battle against the dusky haze. The drowsy drips from the gray-worn awning of the nearby diner set the rhythm of the evening. Each waft of the light breeze brought the faint odor of wet greed. This was Magic City.

My ambling gait broke abruptly when my foot splashed and soaked my sagging black socks. I stepped in a puddle. Couldn't see it; there was a middle-aged gut in the way. Nothing to do about that when you're an egg.

The name's Dumpty. Frank Dumpty. I'm with MCPD.

I've been a detective a long time. Maybe too long. I've seen ugly things in this town. One of the ugliest was two years ago when my kid brother bought the farm. He was on the force, too. Name was Stu, but he had a nickname from making the rounds with a lot of dames. What can I say; Stu was a player.

Jake Spout, captain at the precinct, kept me out of it. Said I was too close. We argued, but deep down I knew it was the right move by Jake, and with a gargoyle, especially your boss, you pick your battles carefully. Still, I never believed the malarkey in the cover report. The one that hit the press. They said he fell. Yeah, right. Stu was a lot of things, but he was agile as a cat. If he was sitting on a wall in the first place—and I have my doubts—losing his balance was out of the question. And if the king sent any horses or men, I'll eat my hat. I tried to get my hands on the real file, but it came up conveniently missing. All I ever dug up was that the doctors tried to get him together again, but there was a piece missing. A big chest piece, about a foot across. No patching that. Not even with magic.

Magic is hard to come by, and expensive. Never mind the name of the city. Magic is what drives this place crazy. When people decide they need it, they'll do anything to get it. That's where the problems start.

Just now, I was making my way to a troll's place. Nasty part of town, but then it's a nasty town. Sure, the society types—the elves, nymphs, fairies—have their fancy digs, but the money comes from the backs of the have-nots, and that makes it all nasty to my way.

The street was an endless string of slums, all in slate gray. Trolls, goblins, ogres. None of them had what you'd call a sense of color. Each door was short and wide, like the tenants, and they all had a single, round window above it. One in five of the windows had glass; the rest were open air. Lots of these folks preferred it that way. The exterior walls were simple panels. No layered siding or shingles or bricks. In the daytime, it was ugly. After dark, even with the streetlamps, it was like trudging through a cave. I'd been here earlier in the day, but finding the same place again was like picking a rock out of a cobblestone road.

I was in the only outfit I ever wore: black pants, white shirt, brown trench coat, blue fedora. My socks and shoes were plain, black, and now, wet. I had a pistol strapped to my hip. Cops weren't allowed to use magic. Go figure. Didn't matter much to me; magic could be unpredictable. I felt safer with a dozen hollowpoints in my Glock.

The house I was looking for was a crime scene a few hours ago. A troll, Andy Bridgeman, got himself splattered all over his nest. It's the kind of case that fades away for most cops, almost as fast as it pops up. No forensic evidence, no apparent motive. No leads. It didn't feel right to me, though. The wife. She kept saying she had no idea how this would happen, but it didn't make sense. Who needs to off a troll in the slum? In his home? She knew something she wasn't saying, and she was too nervous to spit it out. Maybe somebody had her scared.

Maybe if I could talk to her without so many uniforms around, she'd spill it.

I chose a door and knocked. It creaked and swung, and behind it was Marge Bridgeman, Andy's wife. She was about five-two, stocky. Greenish complexion and Neanderthal features, with a unibrow you could use to clean the grill. Not bad for a troll, but she wasn't my type. She was in a simple, one-piece burlap dress, long enough that I didn't see much but bare feet.

"Oh, hello, Detective Dumpty," she said weakly, stepping back a little from the door. "Won't you come in?" She used English for my sake, but with a thick accent of Mountain Troll. She sounded like she was coughing on every word, through a mouthful of pea soup. It didn't help that she'd been crying. I could tell by all the snot coating her chin and the bodice of her dress.

I stepped inside. It was a typical troll place. Dirt floor. Stench like a combination of dead fish and more dead fish. In the middle of the room, a firepit with a metal rod suspended across it for hanging a pot or roasting. Mostly rocks and small plants along the walls around it, except for one of the back corners, where there was a large, round, flat pile of straw and small sticks. The nest. At the moment, most of the sticks were stained red.

Marge waved a gnarled, hairy hand at one of the larger rocks. "Have a seat," she said.

"No thanks, I'll stand," I said.

Marge swung the door closed and stood near it, wringing her hands. "What can I help you with?" She was a trooper. With all she'd just been through, she was still polite and putting up a collected front.

"I'll get to the point," I said. "I know you were nervous when we talked earlier. I get it. Lots of cops around, the shock of finding your husband that way. But people don't get shot up for no reason. If he was just a working stiff like you say—um, sorry about the 'stiff' thing, I didn't mean to—anyway, nobody stands to gain from killing him. Are you sure there isn't something you didn't tell us?"

Marge was staring at the bloody nest. "Not at all. I told you everything I know." That's what she said, but the shakiness was still there, and it wasn't just from grief. She was still plenty nervous to talk about it.

I cut to the chase. "They threatened you, didn't they?"

She looked down and shifted her weight. "I can't ..."

"Trust me," I said. "I know the bad guys are scary. I can help you, but I need you to help me. Give me something here."

"But ... they said ..."

"I know, I know," I said, "but I can stop this. I can keep it from happening to others like your husband. Give me the chance."

Marge looked up into my eyes.

"You were here, weren't you," I said.

"Yes," she answered. "I said I found him, but that's not true. They did it ..." she started tearing up, and her voice waivered. It was hard enough to understand her without that, and now it was nearly impossible.

"They did it right in front of me," she said. "They said he was too far behind, and they don't like people getting behind. They said if I told anybody, the same would happen to me."

"Who's 'they'?"

"Two goblins," said Marge. "I knew one of them. Billy Buckmiser. He's no good, Detective. He's nothing but a magic shark. Andy ..." She trailed off. I could tell she felt guilty for her husband.

"It's OK," I said. I knew of Billy Buckmiser. He was small-time. Liked to act tough. Sometimes he got nasty enough to set an example, and Andy was it, but Billy wasn't the top of the food chain. He was a thug.

"Believe me, Mrs. Bridgeman," I said, "whatever your husband got sucked into, I understand." That's the truth. This damn city—hell, the whole kingdom—drove people down. If you weren't born with a silver spoon, getting one was not in the cards. It made people do desperate things to get ahead. I'd never tell the Captain this, but I actually admired seeing folks with the guts to twist their situation and try to fight a system stacked against them. Black market magic was one of those twists. Sure, the law said buying it was illegal, but to me, the criminals were the pushers. Billy Buckmiser and whoever was pulling his strings.

Marge began crying a little heavier. "It was for our son. It was just for our boy."

"It's OK, Mrs. Bridgeman."

She continued. "All we did was turn some lead into gold. We just wanted him to have a chance. Get an education. Get out of this hell hole. We had to have magic to turn lead into gold. But we couldn't pay it back fast enough, and ..."

"Listen," I said. "You don't need to give me the details. You've been through enough. I know what Billy does, and I know what he did to your husband. I'll take it from here. You don't have to worry about this any more. I promise you that. And thank you, Mrs. Bridgeman. You're doing the right thing. That was very brave."

#

It wasn't far to Billy's. Once I'd pressured a couple stoolies who still owed me, I found the place. Goblins live better than trolls, and Billy lived better than a lot of goblins. Crime pays. For a while. Until somebody skims the scum. Billy was on the edge of the slums, right where he didn't have to feel it all around him but was within easy striking distance of his victims. The house had brown siding, and windows with glass, on the first floor. There was even some space, about five feet, between his house and the buildings on either side. Of course, the space was filled with rusting trash, but it was space just the same. A luxury not many had here.

I held up when I got close enough to scout the place for a second before I moved in, but whatever muscle Billy was using wasn't outside. Not surprising. Customers were too scared of him to begin with, and the beat cops were likely on the take. If Billy was feeling comfortable, that would work in my favor.

I made my way smoothly to the front door. This was no time for knocking. I pulled my Glock, rocked back to get my weight behind my leg, and kicked the door in.

There were only two of them. Billy was on a couch, watching an old tube television, and another goblin thug was in a wooden chair just inside the door. He was there in case of someone like me, but he was way too slow. With my gun drawn, it took a fraction of a second to lay a good pistol-whip. One clout, and he was out cold. A moment later, I was gliding closer to Billy, sights lined up and ready for action. He only got as far as laying his hands on the couch cushions to spring up.

"Freeze," I said. Billy clearly wasn't ready for this. He stopped cold.

"Who the hell are you?" said Billy.

I kept my focus on Billy, but darted glances around the main room. Not much to see; goblins favored hoarding money, not spending it. A plain, wooden coffee table with a newspaper and a couple smut mags. One set of shelves holding a few disgusting knickknacks—maybe trophies from strong-arming the locals—and artwork on the wall. That was unusual for a goblin. It was a painting of some pixies playing poker. Billy had cash, but no taste. Predictable.

The television was distracting. "Turn off the tube," I said. Billy started pushing himself off the couch cushion. "Stop!"

"Well, what the hell," said Billy. "I got no remote. You want the TV off or not?"

"Seriously?" I said. "No remote? What kind of trash hole is this?" In the blink of an eye, I flashed my pistol to the television, blasted out the tube, and had it trained on Billy again.

"Hey!" said Billy.

"Calm down," I said.

"But that's my—"

"Shut up. I didn't come here to jaw about your lame-ass appliances."

"Well, what the hell are you doing here, then?" Billy had a lot of attitude for a thug with no protection and an angry cop in the room.

"It's your lucky day, scum," I said. "I'm not here for you."

"Funny," said Billy, "Nobody else lives here."

"Not so funny, smart guy. I want your boss."

"Boss? You're crazy," said Billy. "I got no boss."

"Skip it, Gobby," I said. "I know you capped Andy Bridgeman, and I know you sold him magic. But you can't make magic, can you, Billy? Who makes your magic?"

"I got nothin' to do with magic," said Billy. "Never touch the stuff."

I lowered my gun and popped a round into Billy's left knee. It came close to tearing his spindly little leg right off. Billy wailed in agony and grabbed his leg. I kept the Glock trained on him; this was a moment he might do something stupid.

"Damn!" said Billy. "Damn you!" He screamed again. "Why'd you do that?" His dark blue-green blood was flowing down his calf.

"There's more where that came from," I said. "I can do this all night."

"OK, OK," Billy said, clutching his wiry thigh and rocking forward and back in pain. "The Caster. I don't know his name. That's all he goes by."

"The Caster?" I said. I'd heard of him. Bad news. Very powerful wizard. "How do you meet him?"

"I don't. He uses messengers. Delivery boys. I've never met him in person."

"How do I contact him?"

"You don't," said Billy. "He contacts you, through the deliveries."

"Is he still in the Crystal Cave?" I'd never been there, but that's where I'd always heard he lived, and wanted to see if Billy would confirm.

"How should I know?" said Billy. "Go there and find out."

I thought I might just have to do that. The Crystal Cave wasn't a fortress, or a secret. Not many saw the inside, though.

"Now, Billy," I said, "there's only one more thing I need you to do for me."

#

The Crystal Cave wasn't a place to barge into by yourself. I needed a team from the precinct. The next morning, I went in to see the Captain. Standard issue police station office. Too small, Spartan furnishings. I knocked.

"Yeah," he barked. I went in and closed the flimsy door, rattling the frosted glass window. Jake Spout was at his desk, a disheveled mess of papers and photos. Gargoyles weren't known for being tidy. There were two armless wooden chairs in front of the desk, facing Jake, and I sat in one of them. Jake was shuffling and reading.

"I did some hunting last night," I said. "I know who's behind the Bridgeman murder."

Without even looking up at me, Jake said, "You're off the case."

"What?" I said. "Off the case? What're you talking about? I'm on a solid track here, Jake. I want to take down The Caster."

Jake chuckled.

"What's so funny?" I asked.

"You think The Caster killed Andy Bridgeman?"

"His goons did," I said, "but I want to take him. I want to go up there with a team and take him."

Jake wasn't chuckling. "Nope. Leave it be."

"So, what, we don't prosecute murders any more?"

Jake locked eyes with me. "I said leave it be. You are off the case."

He meant it. That didn't sit well with me. I took a breath and looked away. "So, who's case is it, then? I'll debrief with them."

Jake was still staring at me. "You're not getting it, Dumpty. Forget the case. Don't push this."

"How can you say that?" I said. "I can't just let it go."

"You really need to," said Jake. "This comes from higher than me. I have no choice, and neither do you. I'm trying to save your skin, here, Dumpty. This is bigger than us. This is how omelets get made. *Let it go*." He looked down at his papers again. "We're done here."

I knew better than to keep arguing. Jake had a tipping point, and if you went past it, there was hell to pay. One time when he went berserk, we practically had to replace the precinct building. Without speaking, I got up and left.

I didn't like where this was going. Where it went, I mean. It was already gone. Jake was usually on the level, but here he was, threatening me. If he was getting pressure on this, it was big. Somebody at headquarters was dirty. Connected to The Caster. That was the only explanation. I had a choice to make. I could save my own skin, or I could keep my promise to Marge Bridgeman.

I spent the rest of the day finding my way to the Crystal Cave.

#

I waited till dark to make a move. The Crystal Cave was near the eastern edge of Magic City, and it wasn't isolated, really. It was just shrouded in mystery and rumors. Downtown, in the slums, it was like a legend. Some people thought it didn't even exist. And that was exactly how The Caster liked it.

The east side was money. Reeked of it. Every day I saw folks like Andy and Marge slaving their lives away with no hope, while these fat cats kicked back and raked it in. The Crystal Cave sat in a sort of crater. There was a big, round ridge of very expensive elf homes, standing like sentinels posted around a deep dip in the land, and there sat the Cave.

Actually, it turns out it wasn't even a cave. It was a cabin. Practically a hut. It was made of stone, though, and the stone was impregnated with crystal. Sparkled a lot. I think it was some kind of shield for magic. The only thing The Caster could be worried about.

I was happy about one thing, at least. The Caster and his Cave had such a reputation, it looked like security was lighter than I expected. Not like he needed any. Nobody was a match for guys like him. Somewhere, there might be wizards who used their magic to help people, but not here. Here, it was a racket.

The last glow of the sun on the clouds faded from orange to black, and at last I had the blessed cover of darkness. My favorite time to work. I found a spot to hide in the shadows of one of the elf homes and scouted for a bit. All I ever saw were two goons outside the front door. A couple ogres with permanent scowls. I imagined worse, but there was no way I could take either of them in a straight fight. And there was no way to know what was inside if I got past them, either. Best I could hope for was that the wizard was alone, figuring he could magic anything that got in, and the ogres were basically an alarm system.

There was a walkway straight down from the ridge to the front door of the Cave, where the ogres were on either side. That was suicide. My only hope was surprise, and the sidewalk was not it. My vantage point was a hundred feet to the side, where it was just a little bit darker. The hill down to the Cave was partly grass, but patchy, and mixed with areas of gravel. I had an idea. It was going to hurt.

I checked my pistol. Still there. I checked my handcuffs. Still there. I checked my resolve. Not as strong as the hardware, but still there. I thought of my chat with Jake. *This is how omelets get made.* I could still pull out. Jake wouldn't be happy I came here, but it would blow over. I could stroll the slums and slap hands.

I just couldn't look in the mirror.

There was a little bottle in my pocket, and I took it out, popped the cork, and downed the contents. I grabbed the belt on my coat and snugged it. This was it. After a deep breath, I leaned forward and to the left, and took off down the hill.

I could only guess the ogres had never seen an egg in a trench coat rolling down a hill, but I got the surprise I was after. I felt some nicks and chips on the way down. If I survived, I'd be sore in the morning. At the last moment, when the ogres realized this wasn't for fun and I wasn't stopping, they began to pull weapons, but by that time I was slamming into them. Into one, anyway. There was lots of cracking going on. Most of it was the ogre's bones against the side of the Cave, but some of it was mine. The pain shot through me like a sword, and I felt a nasty rupture in my right side. Not a clean break. I'd be OK if nothing else happened, but it hurt bad.

The other ogre I managed to catch with my legs and knock off balance while I was slamming into his partner, but it didn't delay him long. I wasn't as quick as Stu used to be, but I rolled to my feet and had my Glock out before he did. One shot and the soft tissue in the ogre's chest got a lot softer. If the ogres were there as an alarm system, I guess it went off.

I blasted another shot into the lock on the door and kicked it in. I'd never done that with a crack in my side, and it hurt like blazes.

Inside, the room felt small. It was about twenty feet square, but cluttered. There were shelves and baskets and stuff everywhere, with glass jars and bottles and bowls all over, filled with liquids and plants and goo. The only place in the room that was clear was the middle, and that's where he stood.

It was The Caster. He was old, with thick, white, firecracker whiskers and deep ravines in the skin across his face. He was barefoot, with a pair of simple, brown slacks and a floppy, white pullover shirt. I half expected a pointy hat, but his thin, matted hair was bare. In an instant, I had the Glock aimed at his torso. He spoke, and his voice was deep and penetrating.

"Welcome, Mr. Dumpty. It's been a long time now, but I've been expecting you."

"Expecting me?" I said.

"I knew you couldn't resist tracking me down sooner or later. It's your nature."

"It's my nature to blow a hole in you if you try anything. You're coming with me."

"Nonsense," said the wizard. "You came because you have a death wish. You came to join your brother."

I looked past him to a shelf on the far wall. There was a curved white piece of shell, about a foot across.

"You," I said. "You bastard."

We were done talking. In a flash, he flicked a finger and a dart of sparkling powder flew across the room. I squeezed my trigger twice as I felt the pressure of the magic powder reach my face. Then, it dissipated, and the wizard was on the floor.

He wasn't dead. Not yet. I pulled the tiny, empty bottle from my pocket and dropped it next to him. It twirled in a little circle on the wooden floor. "Protection potion," I said, "courtesy of Billy Buckmiser. You need more loyal goons, Wizzo."

His eyes were wide with shock for another moment, then closed for good.

#

I set the bottle on a rock in Marge Bridgeman's room, next to the jar and the bowl. Bending over made my side ache, but the crack was on the mend. "I don't know what these do," I said, "but see if you can find somebody to tell you. They came straight from the Crystal Cave, and I'm sure they're loaded with magic. You've already paid more than anybody should for these, so I thought you should have them."

"Thank you, Detective. Thank you so very much."

"My pleasure, Mrs. Bridgeman." I let myself out.

On the street, I stood and inhaled the dankness. Through the gloomy glow of weak neon signs, the thick air swirled with the seedy sounds of sin. I'd have to answer to Jake for going rogue on The Caster, but not now. Now it was just me and Magic City.

The name's Dumpty. Frank Dumpty. I'm with MCPD."

END

Caribou Road

Joe Cron

The droplets of melted snow staggered down the window pane like drunken sailors in a three-legged race. Tiny prisms, they took the flashing neon from across the alley and bent the blue and red until it was almost pretty. Not that anything was pretty in this town. Sure, some glitz and glamour—if you knew where to look—but nothing beautiful. It wasn't pretty being an egg with a badge on the sleazy streets of Magic City.

The name's Dumpty. Frank Dumpty. I'm with MCPD.

Christmas Eve was only a day away, but you'd never know it in this town. Sure, they put up lights, but only so you smile while you're getting reamed. There's big money here. Dirty money. And if you're a little guy, you're only here to do the dirty work for the big guys.

From what I've heard, Santa's an OK sort, but step down the ladder a rung and things get less comfy. The elves are living the good life, too, along with the nymphs and fairies, but somebody's making toys, and it ain't them. The glamour in this town is built on the backs of those toymakers and their lot. Like I said, it's not pretty.

I turned back into the room from the window. Dimly lit place, overcome with gloom. Bundles of sticks leaning up against one wall. Beat-up, sheetless mattress on the floor. Wood stove had a pot on top with various hooves sticking out. Typical working-man's joint. Typical smell, too, like a wet yak that rolled in a compost pile, but this time accented with the earthy bouquet of dead guy.

I was at a demon's place. Christmas demon, name of Knecht Ruprecht. Least ways, he behaved like a demon. Beat kids with wooden sticks. I'm not good with kids, but on the scale of how to treat them, there's not being good with them, and then way far away from that is beating them with sticks.

This guy sure got his comeuppance, though. Looked like a package exploded in his face. A Christmas present, more like. He was sitting at an old, decrepit wooden table in his thread-bare, grey-green hooded robe, right arm still resting on the table, head cocked back with all kinds of shrapnel embedded in it. Bits of cardboard and wrapping paper in front of him.

There were uniforms here, beat cops going through stuff. And there was a lot of it. Ruprecht's place wasn't all that big, but crammed with crap. Sometimes, exactly that. Some things were in crates, some in old trunks and chests, some just sitting out in piles. And off to my left I could swear I saw some kind of slime just flowing down the wall.

I didn't fit in with this crowd. I was round; they were various types of not round. They were mostly on the take, while I bucked the system and stood up for the little guy. They were in uniforms, and my outfit was what it always was: black shoes, socks, and pants, with a white shirt, brown trench coat, and blue fedora.

Key piece of the ensemble was my piece, a Glock filled with hollowpoints, strapped to my hip. The name of the town was Magic City, but most people couldn't afford magic, and cops weren't allowed to use it. Typical. OK with me, though. You weren't supposed to feel good about popping a cap into a bad guy, but I never felt bad about it, and not having magic gave me an excuse to maybe enjoy it a little.

Looking over the scene, I was thinking about how I'd had nothing to eat for hours and it was going to be longer, then wondering how I could be thinking about food in the middle of that stench. Disgusting as a bleu cheese and cow dung sandwich. That an ogre barfed on. With a hair in it. Then my attention turned when I saw a uniform I knew I could trust.

"Baker," I said.

He looked at me and I waved him over.

Baker was a good one. Used to work the king's guard but went MCPD after the business with my brother two years ago. A detective like me, everyone knew him as Humpty, but his real name was Stu. The report was about everything the king's horses and men tried to do to reassemble him, but Baker was on the inside and said it didn't go down like that. Stu was set up to take that fall, with plenty of kickbacks at the palace, and there'd be no putting him together again. Ah, Stu. The sun would shine just a few minutes a day more on this grimy city if you were still around.

Baker was part of a trio of pals that all quit after Stu's murder. Baker came to the force; the other two went into business. One's a butcher, and the other one, believe it or not, makes a living with candlesticks. Some things I'll never understand.

"Yeah, boss," Baker said as he got closer.

"What've we got here?" I said.

"Haven't found much, boss," said Baker.

"Candy canes?"

"Yup," said Baker. "Two candy canes on the table, fresh bootprints in and around the fireplace, some remnant traces of animal hair, and ..." He paused and pointed. "That."

What Baker pointed to was the tabletop. Through the small pools of blood, a trail of it had been pulled out and ended at Ruprecht's index finger.

Written in that trail of blood was the word, SANNTA.

#

My boss, Jake Spout, sat at his desk among the piles of papers, sandwich wrappers, and ashtrays. It was tough to get a gargoyle to listen about the dangers of lung cancer. His office was classic cop-shop stuff. A desk, two chairs facing it, and a coat rack, all sitting on top of old, yellow linoleum. Walls were tacky paneling with a few pictures of Jake with dignitaries.

I was in one of the chairs, arguing with the gargoyle. All too common, but never a comfortable place to be.

"You are not going after the fat man," said Jake.

"The hell," I said.

"Don't play tough with me. There's no case."

"No case!" I said. There was nothing but case. All I had was case. The evidence made a case like no case that was ever cased.

Truth was, Knecht Ruprecht wasn't the first murder. There were three now. All three were Christmas demons. First was Krampus. Messiest crime scene I've seen in a while. Then came Grýla. Dear Lord, what a household. Seventy-two kids and a Yule Cat. Thank God for the uniforms to do all the interviews. Even then it took two days.

And with all three, the same evidence. Had the animal hairs analyzed each time, and each time they turned out to be reindeer.

"I've got candy canes, bootprints in the fireplace, and reindeer DNA with every murder," I said. "What do you suppose those have in common?"

"There were candy canes?"

"Yeah," I said. "Candy canes."

"So, what?"

"Well, who do you know that gives out candy canes?"

"Hm. Let me think," said Jake. "Maybe, anybody who buys them."

"Sure, boss. Knecht Ruprecht and Krampus are out buyin' candy canes. Hand 'em out to the kids between beatings."

"And why exactly would Claus go leave an exploding box to kill somebody and then hey, here's a couple candy canes while I'm here?"

"Maybe it was an accident," I said. "Fell out of his pocket."

"What, you think he just walks around poopin' out candy canes?"

"How am I supposed to know how it works?"

"Leave the fat man alone," said Jake.

"But—"

Jake slammed his hand down on the desk. And when a gargoyle does that, you wonder how the desk stays standing. "You really want to do this? After all he's done for you?"

"Captain, don't make this personal."

"Loyalty means nothin' to you?"

That hit close to home. And Jake knew it would. Loyalty meant everything to me, which is why it stung so hard that Claus could have gone off the rails like this.

"Look," I said. "I can't let emotions into this. Fats and I had an arrangement. That's all. I spent the year being good, and he brought me presents at Christmas."

"That's all it was?" said Jake.

"Don't get me wrong; the presents are terrific and all. That fake badge that squirts water? Genius. Had you laughing for a week."

"Oh Jeez, don't get me started," said Jake. "That was hysterical."

"But it can't sway this case. Everything points to Santa."

Jake pushed himself up from his desk and leaned back in his chair. "Well, let's talk about that."

"What do you mean?"

"Every victim wrote his name in blood, right?"

It was true. All three victims spelled it out in blood. Damnedest thing I ever saw.

"Right," I said. "Could there be a stronger message for who the killer is?"

"But they all spelled it with an extra 'N?'"

I thought about that some more. It's true. They had all written SANNTA.

"Yeah," I said. "So, what?"

"So, what are the odds that three different people make the same spelling error while they're dying?"

"Well, I wouldn't have figured it was very good," I said, "but here we are."

"No," said Jake, leaning forward again and pointing a finger at me. "It means it's somebody else. Figure out who this Sannta is, with his extra 'n,' and you'll have your killer. In the meantime—"

"I know, I know," I said, "leave the fat man alone." I thought for a second. Even if I don't go after Santa, there's still three murders to solve. "So who else have I got?"

"Nobody. Everybody. I don't care. Just keep Claus out of it. If I hear you've been to the north pole, there'll be hell to pay."

There were four huge flagpoles in Magic City, one at each side of town. Santa's cottage was right at the base of the north pole. But I'd keep my cool and steer clear. For now.

#

I needed a lead. Somebody on the inside. Jake was right; the evidence was just a little too convenient. But if it was a setup, who has access to reindeer DNA? Maybe an elf, but I didn't know any I could trust. I'd have to go straight to the delivery team. The stables.

I'd been there before. The stables weren't my favorite place. Reminded me of days gone by—way, way by—when I was a uniform on mounted patrol. Police budgets being what they were, we didn't have any saddles made for eggs. Had a bad experience. Got transferred to the motorcycle unit, which was right up my alley. Great days on the sled.

The stables were just outside of town, on the west side. In the city, traffic and bodies kept things a little warmer, and the streets didn't often hold snow for long before it turned into sloppy, grey slush. Out here, though, everything was white with December snow. Some years I went the whole winter without seeing the white countryside. Seemed somehow fake, like a painting. A pretty veneer masking Magic City's underbelly.

It wasn't a huge property. There was a ranch house, barn, a corral attached to that, and not much else. The reindeer were the only ones here. Santa didn't like them mingling with less exclusive livestock. Actually, I heard Claus wasn't that elitist, but the elves coached him into some of this stuff. No trouble believing that.

As I approached on foot up the dirt driveway, I could see seven reindeer outside in the corral. One still in the stable, then. There used to be a ninth, but they had a falling out a ways back. The Nose. He didn't stay here anymore. He lived in a cabin out at the end of Caribou Road. Nobody had seen him in quite a while now.

A few more steps, and I could smell the place. Nasty. Decaying worms on top of goblin farts. Worse than Knecht Ruprecht's.

OK, not really. Ruprecht's place was unbelievably disgusting. He wins. But this was still really, really bad.

I got closer to the corral, and I could tell the reindeer were pensive. Jumpy, and obviously talking quickly to each other. If ever somebody was getting their story straight, that was it.

They'd picked a spokesman, too, and when I was within earshot, he spoke.

"Hey there," the reindeer said. I just kept walking closer. "Name's Dancer."

I moved off the driveway and trudged through the ankle-deep snow until I came up to the wooden rails of the corral. Dancer was about eight feet away, the rest of them more than twice that. I flashed my badge. "Name's—"

"Dumpty," said Dancer. "We know you. Your reputation precedes."

"I don't even want to know what that's about," I said, "but if you get rumors out here, then you must know about the recent murders."

"The three Christmas demons? Yeah, we heard."

"What exactly did you hear?" I said.

"We heard three Christmas demons got killed."

"And?"

"And what?" said Dancer. I never interviewed a reindeer for a case before, and this guy was clamming up good. Maybe too good.

"Oh, come on," I said. "You got nothing to do out here but gossip. You sure there hasn't been some talk about who might want to go and do something that awful?"

"You're the famous detective, with the even more famous brother. Don't you have any evidence or something to help you get your man?"

"Oh, plenty of that," I said. Looks like the reindeer didn't chat to get their story straight. They were busy deciding there was no story at all. "But I'm missing a motive. If you want to know who-done-it, you figure out why-done-it, and you're most of the way there."

"Sounds reasonable," said Dancer. "But why ask a reindeer?"

My shoes weren't made for snow. My feet were cold and wet, and I was getting nowhere fast. "No reason. Just thought you might've caught wind of some Christmas rumors and might want the killer to come to justice."

"Haven't heard a thing," he said. He gestured with his head toward the rest of the reindeer behind him. "Neither have they."

"Have it your way," I said, turning to leave. "But I find out later that you knew something and didn't tell me, it's obstruction."

"I'll keep that in mind," said Dancer.

Walking back toward the driveway, I came close enough to the barn to notice that the big door was cracked open a few feet. It was closed when I got there.

"Psst. Hey, Egg." It was a woman's voice. And even with just those words, it was smooth as silk. I moved slightly closer to the barn.

"Yeah, Egg, over here," she said. I strode more confidently toward the open door.

"Don't come in," she said. I stopped just outside.

"I can't see you," I said.

"Right."

"Unless I miss my guess, you're—"

"Vixen," she said. That golden voice was enough to thaw you in the snow. "You should know something."

"I just got the cold shoulder from Dancer and the crew. Why would you be telling me anything I can believe?"

"Your brother," she said. "I ... liked him."

Made sense. She was Vixen, after all, and everybody knew Stu got around. You don't get his nickname in Sunday school.

"I'm sorry about what happened," she said. "I want to help."

Finally, somebody that is interested in punishing criminals. "Thanks," I said. "I don't get much of that."

"You need to know about Sannta," she said.

"I know plenty, already," I said. "What's new?"

"Not him. The one with two 'n's."

My ears perked on that one. This two-"n"ed Sannta was a complete mystery.

"What about him?" I said.

"Spirits come in pairs," said Vixen. "Good and bad, yin-yang, up-down, whatever."

"OK. Like reciprocal energies."

"Oh, honey, don't hurt your brain like that. Good and bad."

"My brain's just fine, but all right. Good and bad. Got it."

"Santa, with one 'n,' is good," she said.

"But there's a twin?"

"Not exactly. The spirit—yes, that's an evil twin. The body? Not so much."

I was moving around some, trying to get some kind of a look inside the barn. If nothing else, I wanted a glance at the dame attached to that voice. No luck, though. "So, who?"

"Think on it," she said. "Who might have access to candy canes, reindeer DNA, and maybe a pair of Santa's old boots for making prints?"

"Oh, my God," I said. "You mean—"

"Ever been out to Caribou Road?" said Vixen.

Caribou Road. Home of The Nose. Some said Rudolph could make the red glow so bright it would burn your eyes right out. Yeah, seems it was time to go out to Caribou Road. But I had one other stop to make on the way.

#

It was a nice cabin. All wood, in a warm tone. No glass in the windows. The open-air concept was common in Magic City. Property was a good size, too, off the end of the road, and a long road at that. Almost out in the country. Private, with a lot of large pine trees. Perfect for somebody with a schnoz that might disturb the neighbors.

I had Baker with me. I often went solo if the mission wasn't by the book, but no reason to go it alone this time, since I wasn't disobeying Jake's orders. Yet.

It was dark out, but not so much as it might have been, owing to the snow. Seemed to reflect the city glow, even though we weren't in the thick of it. Baker and I started up the path to the front door, then split up and veered off, circling to case the joint. The red glow inside told us we were at the right place.

That was The Nose.

I should've gotten some different shoes.

I was along the side of the house, way past having visual contact with Baker, when I remembered to put on my sunglasses. We both had extra dark sunglasses with us, on a count of people going blind if The Nose cranks up the power on that beak.

Made it to the back of the house. No Baker. I wasn't sure what could be keeping him, but there was no noise, either, so I wasn't too concerned. I found a door in back. I pulled my Glock and crept toward it. I was only two steps away when I heard The Nose. A gravelly voice, like he'd had a few too many cigarettes.

"I hear ya, Dumpty."

I froze. "No, you don't."

"Smell ya, too."

"Liar."

"Maybe."

"Why'd you do it?" I said.

"Do what?"

"Sure, wise guy. Play dumb. But I'm coming in to arrest you, and you know full well why, Sannta." I said it with some extra time on the "n"s so he would know I meant the two "n"s.

"Fine, so I didn't smell ya. But I knew it was you. I knew you're the only one who would figure that out."

"I didn't figure it out," I said. "Somebody told me."

"Whatever," said The Nose. "You figured out that those demons didn't write that name in the blood. I did."

I smiled. "You wrote that name in the blood?"

"Skip it," said The Nose. "We're both here now."

"We are. But you still haven't told me why."

There was some silence.

After a moment, the reindeer spoke again. "Everybody punishes the misfits."

"So, what?"

"I want them to go free. To be rewarded. To thrive!"

"What's that got to do with the likes of Krampus?"

"Ha!" said The Nose. "Everybody thinks somebody like Krampus is the opposite of Santa. Santa good, Krampus bad. But think about it, Dumpty. Santa rewards good children, and Krampus punishes bad ones. They may be two sides, but they're on the same coin. I want to reward the bad ones. You see, Dumpty, the opposite of Santa isn't a demon with the same sense of justice. The opposite of Santa is Sannta."

He said it with some extra time on the "n"s so I would know he meant the two "n"s.

"And I," he continued, with an air of pride in his voice, "am Sannta."

Again with the extra "n" time.

"I'm coming in now," I said.

"Help yourself," said The Nose.

I stepped up and opened the door, gun raised and sunglasses firmly on my face. The cabin was one room. To my left, and down the side wall, was a kitchen area. In front of me, a couch with an end table, facing me. To my right, a rock and a pile of straw. Everything fit except the couch. Why does a reindeer need a couch?

Behind that couch stood The Nose. Schnoz was glowing, but clearly not at full power. Just enough to light the room, and it was the only light in the room, bathing everything in red.

I got inside the door and stopped. "Hm. What's with the furniture?" I said. "Somethin' about reindeer I don't know?"

"It's not mine. Belonged to the ogre I bought the place from, and I haven't gotten rid of it, yet. You want a couch?"

"I'll pass," I said. Still had the Glock trained on him. "You're under arrest."

The Nose doused the glow. The room was quickly and utterly black. I heard some scuffling of hooves, but even protected behind the sunglasses my eyes weren't yet adjusted enough to make out movement.

Then, a hoof hit my left shoulder. Hard. Not quite hard enough to crack my shell, but it shook everything good, and both my gun and my sunglasses went flying.

Now was the time I was going to get full power from The Nose.

In the same moment that The Nose turned everything up full blast, Baker came bursting in the side door. Turns out there were three entrances. The Nose was on my side of the couch now, and Baker was behind it, sunglasses on. Good man.

The Nose turned toward Baker and charged around the couch. I closed my eyes, but that wasn't going to be enough. The light was so intense I could feel it through my shell. This was powerful enough to cook me if I was in it too long.

But The Nose going after Baker gave me a moment. The moment I needed. And with The Nose moving away from me, his body was between me and that honker. I was in a bit of shadow. Not a second to lose.

I reached into my coat pocket and pulled out a coiled rope, one with a faint glow of blue. As The Nose made it to the far side of the couch and closed in on Baker, I took a quick step directly toward the couch, then leapt up on it.

With a single bounce, I catapulted in a somersault over the top of The Nose's back. The rope was tied as a lasso, and as I vaulted over The Nose I dropped the looped end over him. As if it knew where to go, the rope flowed down over his antlers, head, and body. By the time it reached around his legs, I was landing on the floor. I tugged on the end of the rope I still held, and it closed tightly around all four hooves.

The Nose fell over and slid a few feet. I was near the end of the kitchen counter now, and as I closed my eyes again I grabbed a towel and tossed it in Baker's direction. Within a few seconds, everything went dark.

After another moment, a feeble white light came on. Baker had a flashlight. Good man.

I stood up and did my best to survey the situation. I was a little out of breath, and a little nauseous from the light. My eyes stung, too, but I could see. And what I could see was Baker kneeling over The Nose, hog-tied with a towel around his sniffer. Everything was going to be all right.

"Ever seen a rodeo, Baker?" I said.

"Nope."

"Me, neither. But that might be kind of how it goes."

"I doubt that very much, boss."

"Me, too," said The Nose. "A magic rope? Isn't that outside department policy?"

"You do what you have to," I said. "You can thank Santa for that."

No long 'n' that time.

"Yeah," said The Nose, "that's about his speed."

"An early Christmas gift," I said.

"Nice one, too," said Baker.

"Well, it's no squirting badge," I said, "but it came in handy."

I took a few steps back around the couch so I was between it and the back door, and I took a deep breath of the cross-breeze through the windows. "Call it in, Baker."

I stepped out the back door and onto the white lawn. Didn't even mind the snow freezing my feet, for the moment. I looked around at the natural trees I see so rarely, and thought of the next day. I'd have the Captain screaming across his desk at me—again—but as always, it didn't matter. Jake had to do that stuff to support policy, but he knew I got things done. He's always known this city needs me out here.

I took a deep, chilly breath, then let it out in a rush. This one was special. This one sent a message: no matter how powerful or dangerous you are, the day you think you're above the law is the day I set you straight. Nobody gets a free pass. Not in Magic City.

The name's Dumpty. Frank Dumpty. I'm with MCPD.

END

The Murders in the Room Org

Joe Cron

The evening air was cool and heavy, and after the rain, glints from the scattered streetlights made everything the same, as if the entire town was an abyss that could swallow people whole.

There was a strong smell like gargoyle manure. Pungent, but some would say not all that far off the general murk in the dank pathways of Magic City.

"What're you showin' me here, Sergeant?" I said to a nearby uniform. Sergeant Flargoyle. There was one other, but Flargoyle was closer, and more engaged.

"Gargoyle manure," said Flargoyle. Made sense, if sense had anything to do with it. And the sense of smell sure as hell did.

"You sure it's gargoyle, Flargoyle?" I said.

He was. I knew that. I just couldn't walk away from that situation without saying it.

"Sure as eggs are round," said Flargoyle. It was a ridiculously lame comeback.

For starters, eggs aren't round. We're ovoid. Unless you're maybe looking from the top or bottom, but Flargoyle didn't say, "Sure as eggs are round from the top or bottom." And it's not even a known expression. In fact, I was beginning to think this wasn't even the first time Flargoyle had heard a gargoyle/Flargoyle reference. Sure, he was trying to be funny, but too hard. I was the only egg on the force, but even as a detective, I still took the occasional shot like that from a smartass.

The name's Dumpty. Frank Dumpty. I'm with MCPD.

Got to admit, to look at me, "ovoid" isn't the first word to come to mind. I was in my standard get-up: black pants, socks, and shoes; white shirt with red suspenders and no tie—against dress code at the precinct, and the Captain gives me grief about it, but ever since the thing with the nest and the griffin, no ties—with a brown trench coat and blue fedora. Glock at the hip.

It's true I was the only egg on the force, but it wasn't always that way. There were brighter days. I had a brother, Stu. Toughest, smartest cop I ever met. Horniest, too, and it got him a nickname that stuck forever, but the poor bastard got set up on that wall. Great fall, my ass. I tracked down a wizard named The Caster, and he paid the price, but not before he took Stu from us. Better days.

The manure was resting in a few scattered clumps on the wet sidewalk of one of the seedier sections of town. Mostly tenements here. Magic City had its glamour, but not around here. Off somewhere, far away, where elves and fairies use magic and drink toasts in finery from the sweat of the poor sods in these tenements. Trolls, ogres, goblins, mostly. The working stiffs. Doing the ugly business in an ugly town.

Here, streets were cramped, and door after door the same. Short, wide, and rough, like the tenants. Most windows were open-air. For the best, really. But it made the place feel more like caves than housing. The building we were standing at was the cornerstone of the neighborhood: the Org Hotel.

"I'm homicide, Flargoyle," I said, "and I assume the manure is dead, but unless somebody killed it, I don't get why I'm here smelling it."

Without speaking, Flargoyle slowly pointed up.

I looked, and ten feet above us, resting precariously on a thick cement ledge, was the charred, smoldering carcass of a newly dead gargoyle.

"Well, if that don't beat all," I said.

Flargoyle gestured faintly toward the other uniform, who had a phone to his ear. "Targoyle called in some equipment to get him down."

"Who?"

Flargoyle tossed his head toward the uniform. "Targoyle."

"Oh. Sorry. For a second there I thought you said 'Pargoyle,' and that would've been odd."

"Right. He's Nineteenth Precinct, isn't he?"

"Yup." Flargoyle and I were both Twentieth. "You said we had a crane coming?"

Flargoyle pointed down the street. There were headlights I took to be the crane truck. I took right.

It took time to get the body down, taking time I didn't want to take, but time takes its own time sometimes, and this time was one of those time-taking times I didn't take time for.

In time, the body was down, plopped on the sidewalk near the manure, and ready for examination. A normal gargoyle's body isn't exactly what I would call sleek, but this one was like a cremated pretzel, way past how burned you might think an overdone pretzel might still taste good. Way past.

The thing that hit me, though, was the face. Less burned than the torso, and I kind of wished it was more. This goyle's face was no picnic to begin with, but I'd worked with goyles for a while—the Precinct Captain, Jake Spout, was a gargoyle—and it never occurred to me before that I'd never actually seen one … scared.

Weird as it was, the look on this face was stark terror. He didn't die from the fear; there was plenty else for that. Everything was pretty well incinerated, but the face said he died petrified.

Something scared the crap out of this gargoyle.

Then killed it. I'd never seen either of those happen before.

"Get this carcass down to the morgue," I said.

"You might rue that," said Flargoyle.

"I might what?"

"Rue, sir. You might rue that."

"As in …"

"Regret," said Flargoyle. "Regret for a decision chosen poorly."

"Then say so, for God's sake. Everybody knows the only thing that ever gets rued is the day. Everybody knows that, Flargoyle." I don't know why Flargoyle kept trying to make some kind of impression on me, but he wouldn't like the kind he was making.

"Well, sir, it was only—"

"Oh, I'm going to 'rue' the day I send this carcass to the morgue, is that it? Why not just call it the Morgue of Rue?"

"I only meant, Detective, that sending this carcass away might prove to be premature," said Flargoyle.

He may have been trying to help. I couldn't tell. If he was, he had a hell of a way of showing it. But I didn't have much to lose by humoring the guy.

"OK, I'll bite," I said. "Why would I let this body stay here?"

"Because it's not the only one."

#

Inside the hotel and up two flights of stairs, I stood in the wide hallway of the area they called their Regal Suites. A little pretentious for my taste, given that the overworn wooden floors, peeling wallpaper, and dingy lighting were the same here as in the rest of the hotel. Mixes of grey and brown everywhere, in bizarre patterns that had to be horrifically ugly the day it was built, with no renovations since then. The smell was like they took stale air and locked it in a cave for a million years. Every move made creaks and groans, to where you half expected the floor to wake up and complain. Now and again, a thud or maybe a faint scream from the floor below. The kind that makes you think they found something that shouldn't be in a hotel room.

The Org Hotel was owned and operated by three sphinxes, in this case sisters, but they were pretty reclusive. It wasn't their only property, and they were all in the slums. On the surface, nothing untoward, but just below it, toward and untoward aplenty. I'd never had a full-on run-in with them, but I'd been close enough to it to know you stay on the surface if you can. If you ran afoul of the Org sisters, they might, as the expression went around there, "ask a riddle," and I never heard of anyone having an answer.

Their names weren't actually all Org. Only one, but that was the name they all agreed to use for the hotel, so it kind of stuck as a family name. Here with the Regal Suites, though, you saw all three, because they named them after the sisters.

Flargoyle followed me up. The stairs were wide, with a bit of styling, and at the top was the hallway, the main part of which was large and had gently curved walls guiding a visitor off to the right and down the hall. From the top of the stairs, the first thing on the left was the stairway up to the fourth and final floor above. That was the convention hall, but it hadn't been used for many years.

Straight ahead from the stairs, across that main hallway, was a pair of heavy-looking wooden doors, closed. Slightly down the hall, but on the same side, was another set of similar doors, also closed. At the end of the hall, forty feet away, was another set of those doors, both open.

There was another uniform already up here, but down the hall. Flargoyle was to my left, and he gestured across me that direction.

"Bodies are down there, Detective," he said.

"In which room?" I said.

"Well, the three Regal Suites have the sisters' names."

"Right."

"Florg, Schmorg, and Org."

"Excuse me?" I said.

"Florg, Schmorg, and Org."

"One of them is 'Schmorg?'"

"Yes, sir," said Flargoyle.

"How unfortunate."

"Why, sir?"

I had a serious issue with words and names that start with "schm," but I didn't trust Flargoyle to accept the nuances of my take on this struggle for meaning in the bowels of Magic City.

"Read some Descartes," I said, "and get back to me on that." Sometimes if you want respect, you have to throw these uniforms a curve ball. Descartes had nothing to do with it, but Flargoyle didn't know that.

"Um, Detective, I'm pretty sure Descartes has nothing to do with it."

I feigned indignance. "Wouldn't you like to know."

"Not in the least."

I paused.

"So, the rooms," I said.

"Right," said Flargoyle, perking up. "Three rooms. I hadn't mentioned it yet, but there are actually crime scenes in all three. First one here in front of us is the Room Florg. There were two rapes in there. Second in the middle is the Room Schmorg. Several burglaries in that one. Murders were in the third one, farther down."

"The Room—"

"Detective!" came a woman's voice from down the hall. It was the other uniform, and she was standing in the open doorway. "Glad you could make it, sir. Have a look here."

I knew her. This dame was a real go-getter. Name of McGillicuddyargoyle. Harpy from the depths of the city's gutters, she was trying to make a difference, trying to bring some sense to these mean streets. I wasn't much for harpies, but if I were, I'd ... still probably not have anything to do with her. Harpies were just ... yeah. But there was a part of her I recognized. And admired.

I called down the hall. "In a sec." I turned back to Flargoyle. "I'm not vice or burglary, but is anyone working the cases in these other rooms?"

"I believe so, sir. I believe Detective Flumpty is working the first room, and Detective Schmumpty is—"

"Wait," I said. "Are you serious right now?"

"About what, sir?"

"That name. You have got to be kidding me right now."

"What I'm telling you right now," said Flargoyle, "is that the detective's name is Schmumpty."

"Unbelievable."

"Is there a problem, Detective?"

"Not one you can solve." I made my way purposefully down the hall to the doorway and spoke to the other uniform. "So, what's the situation here, McGillicuddyargoyle?"

"Please, sir, you can just call me McGargoyle. Everyone does."

"Fine," I said, "but don't ever use that around the Captain."

"Oh, there have already been several instances, I'm afraid."

"Really?" She clearly registered the curious surprise on my face.

"Trust me, Detective, it was sufficiently unpleasant."

"I've no doubt," I said. "Well, then, McGargoyle, there were murders in this room?"

"Indeed there were," she said, turning into the room. She swept an arm across in front of her. She was large—taller than I was—and had the bird thing going on, but her wings were more like gnarly, grey arms with huge, deep brown feathers extending, so despite her general physical nastiness, the gesture was fairly grand as she spoke. "Everywhere."

This girl was not kidding. The place looked like a whirling dervish came through with a flamethrower. The spacious room, as decrepit as everything else in the building, had a couch to the left, then a desk, then a stone arch to the bathroom. Furnishings were in dark wood, with upholstery and other fabrics in red or orange. Front and center in the large space was an enormous bed with an ornate canopy. Might have actually been decent at some point. To the right, a dresser with a missing drawer, a vanity table, and two chairs. Between the chairs was an open-air window with rough, wooden framing.

All of it was charred. To some degree, at least. "And they call us the heat," I said. Nothing was still actively smoldering, but the smells were of pretty fresh burns. And a mix of burns: wood, cloth, plastic ... and meat.

I stepped into the room and began looking around. Surfaces were charred, but not frames. Top of the desk, but not the lower half of the legs. Some parts of the floor were burned, but not many.

And there were definitely murders in that room. Moving slowly, I started to the left and surveyed the carnage in a clockwise sweep. On the couch, the twisted, charred remains of a goblin. Another crispy goblin on the floor next to the desk.

Further around the room, on the floor between the bed and the bathroom arch, two overheated trolls, with some dice, bones, and a few other trinkets nearby. Gamers.

Nobody on the bed, but the blankets went up. One more fried goblin on the floor next to an incinerated chair.

Then I looked out the window and down. Sure enough, the dead gargoyle was scared witless and trying to get away. He was directly below.

I turned back into the room and strolled back across toward the gamers. When I reached the middle of the room, an old, gnarled elf came in, approaching me slightly and wearing a bright blue hotel staff uniform. She came up to my shoulder, but used to be taller.

The elf looked at me and pointed toward the gamers and other bodies on that side of the room. "Can I cover them now?"

Elves had magic. Most creatures had to use magic from something else, like a potion or enchanted object, but elves had it inside them. One of the main reasons they were in the mansions while the backbreakers were in the slums. If this one was working at a hotel like the Org, something had gone horribly wrong. It seemed insensitive to mention it, but I did, anyway.

"What's an elf like you doing working at a place like this?" I said.

"What's an ovoid like you doing belittling an elf?" she said.

Trust an elf to know her shapes. "Just doing my job."

"Isn't that a little insensitive?" she said.

"Seemed like it," I said, "but I can't play favorites when I'm on a case."

"Well, I'm just doing my job, too," she said. "Observe."

She took a couple steps toward the charred bodies, but wasn't very close to them. She pulled out a tiny swatch of brown cloth, barely the size of a couple fingertips. She licked her thumb, pressed it to the cloth, and tossed it forward.

The cloth immediately exploded into a huge, brown sheet that covered almost that whole side of the room. The couch and desk, with the burned goblins, and the whole scene of the gamers on the floor, were all easily enveloped by the furling cloth.

"Impressive," I said, "but I didn't give you permission."

"I made assumptions," she said.

"Let me make one. You're Principal Staff."

"No, I'm Esmerelda. And you're annoying."

"No, I'm Dumpty. Frank Dumpty. I'm with MCPD. And you're going to tell me how you're allowed to use magic here."

"Fine," she said. "No skin off my nose."

Good thing, too. I could see the skin on her nose, and it could stay there forever, for all I cared. I could never understand how nose skin ever became a thing in the first place.

"Yeah, I'm Principal Staff," she said. "I'm amazed you even know what that is."

"Well, you'd be amazed at what I know," I said.

"That's what I just said," she said.

"And you would be," I said.

Principal Staff was a designation created by the City Council. The country had a king, and the king lived in Magic City, but the city's government was a mayor and a council. Long ago, the City Council decided businesses of certain types were allowed to have one employee with inherent magic. Elves, fairies, witches, and wizards were the bulk of them. That employee was labeled Principal Staff. Hotels were one of the businesses that could use one.

All the upscale places had them, but Principal Staff was notoriously expensive, so they were more like a legend in the Twentieth Precinct. Esmerelda was right—most people around there wouldn't know what it is.

"One thing I know," I said, "is there's no way the Org can afford you."

"True enough," said Esmerelda. "The city pays my salary." She flashed me a canary-eating cat grin and turned to the other side of the room.

McGargoyle was over there, and she waved me to her.

"May I make an observation, Detective?" she said.

"Sure." What did I have to lose? An ambitious uniform might be nosing around a little more closely than some, and see something the rest of us miss.

"The way the char marks sweep away from the burns," said McGargoyle.

"I know," I said. "Almost spooky, isn't it?"

"I've analyzed the residues of—"

"It's as if they didn't just burn," I said. "It's like wind."

"Every creature has a signature—"

"As if the murderer were somehow yelling at them. Screaming their anguish through the flames."

"Detective?" said McGargoyle.

"What is it?" I said.

"These people were all killed by a fire-breather."

"Nonsense."

"No, I mean it," said McGargoyle.

"Me, too."

"The sweeping char marks—"

"Are very clever and artistic, but trust me, McGargoyle, it was a flamethrower or a fan or something."

"Sir, I'm not certain if you're aware—"

"There hasn't been a fire-breather in Magic City since before you were born."

"Well, sir," said McGargoyle, "there is now. And it's a goat."

#

"It's the damndest thing, Jake," I said, pacing around in short, excited steps. I was in my boss' office. Jake Spout, Captain of the Twentieth Precinct, and a gargoyle. There were pros and cons to all that.

"She's a harpy," I said. "Ever worked with a harpy before, Jake? Damndest thing. It's like she can taste a creature's essence."

"Oh, yeah?" said Jake, sitting at his old, often-rebuilt desk, behind a mess of papers and photos. There were goyles with wings and those without. Those without were the larger of the two, and that was Jake. Grey, stony, and larger than life behind that desk, looking like he could flick it away with a fingernail.

"Jake, I don't have to tell you, but I will, because if I don't, you won't know, so in a way I do have to tell you, that if what that harpy told me is true, it's very telling."

Jake leaned back a little in his chair, the furniture screeching under far too many years of gargoyle. "Do tell."

There were two armless chairs in front of Jake's desk, facing it, and I sat in the one on the left.

"A fire-breather, Jake."

Jake rocked forward again and placed his elbows on the desk, on top of scattered reports and files. I could smell him. Smelled like earth. "A what?"

"It's been how many years?" I said.

"Not enough."

"And get this: the harpy said this fire-breather is a goat."

Jake bolted upright.

"What is it?" I said.

Jake slouched back down. "Nothing."

"A sudden itch in your back?"

"Something like that. Uh, how did she know?"

I stood up and started my little pacing steps behind the two chairs again. "That was the tasting thing, Jake. It's so weird. She said creatures leave their essence on everything they touch, and harpies can taste it later. I asked if it tasted like chicken, but I don't think she's ever seen one. Anyway, it's in your breath, too, so when a fire-breather burns something, their essence is in the char. There were six victims in that room, and all six had essence of goat in their ashes."

"In a room? What room?" said Jake.

"The one at the end of the hall," I said.

"I've been in that hotel," said Jake. "There's the Room Schmorg, the Room Florg, and the Room—"

"Wait. No. You switched them. The Room Florg is the first one. Anyway, five bodies in the room, a sixth that climbed outside, and all six with crispy goat."

"Gosh," said Jake, using a word that unintentionally signaled plain as day that everything following was utter malarkey. "I've never heard of a fire-breathing goat."

I stopped pacing. "Sure about that?"

Jake's manner quickly warned me off. "I said so, didn't I?"

"Fine, if you say so."

"I do say so. I did. I said so and said I said so, so yeah, I say so."

"Fine. So says the so-sayer."

Jake paused. "But I do have a lead you can chase."

I took a step toward Jake's desk, intrigued. "Oh?"

"There's a guy I know," said Jake. "Rap sheet a mile long. Deals in creatures. Any fire-breather is obviously illegal, and something that rare is almost certainly in this guy's arena."

"Sounds good," I said. "Can I take McGargoyle?"

Jake exploded with a single syllable that nearly blew the frosted window right out of the office door behind me. "Who?!"

"Um … uh … McGillicuddyargoyle, sir. Captain."

"That's better. And yes. Sounds like she has unique skills that suit this case."

"That'll suit a lot of cases," I said. "She's a good one, and she's fighting the fight. She'll be an asset."

"Good enough." Jake grabbed a nearby pencil and looked at a random document on his desk.

"Um, sir?" I said.

Jake looked up. "You're still here?"

"Who do I need to go see?"

"Ah, right," said Jake. "Phil Schmargoyle."

"Excuse me?"

"You need to find Phil Schmargoyle," said Jake.

"Phil. Schmargoyle. Seriously?"

Jake sat back a little and began to chuckle slightly, as if ready to announce his charade, then rocked forward and slammed a fist on the desk so hard it should have gone through the floor. Would've, too, if not for reinforcements installed after previous incidents.

Jake's bellow nearly shoved me across the room. "Am I laughing? Huh? The man's name is Schmargoyle, Dumpty! Get used to it."

I paused while the echoes died down. "Oh, I'm already used to it," I said, feeling like there must now be something I needed to brush off myself. "I just hate words that start with 's-c-h-m.'"

Jake sat back a touch and his breathing finally stopped making the walls pulsate. "Why on Earth ..."

"With any other word, you want to poo-poo it, you just say it again only starting with 's-c-h-m.' If you don't want pizza, you say, 'Pizza, schmizza.'"

"No, I say, 'I don't want pizza.'"

"Yeah, well, Jake, the rest of the world says, 'Pizza, schmizza.'"

"I highly doubt that."

Jake was a fine cop, but out of touch.

"Anyway," I said, "if the word already starts like that, you're screwed. You don't want Schmekel Pastrami? Tough. If you just say, 'Schmekel Schmekel,' you're just repeating yourself with no real indication that you don't actually prefer the pastrami, and you sure can't say, 'Schmekel, Schmeschmekel,' or you sound lobotomized."

"You just said it."

"Well, I know how to make it sound smooth, but it's still ridiculous, Jake, and makes your tongue do weird things."

Jake paused. "So that's when you just say, 'I don't want Schmekel Pastrami.'"

"Which is crazy," I said. "Have you had it?"

Jake started to open a drawer on his left.

"Exactly," I said. Jake paused, then closed the drawer. "But whatever, Jake. A name's a name. So where's this Phil guy?"

"Which Phil?"

"What do you mean, 'Which Phil?'" I said.

"There's more than one Phil in the world, Dumpty."

I wiggled a finger in a thinking motion. "Well, yeah, but ... the one you were just talking about."

"I was just talking about one?"

"Oh, for God's sake, Jake, fine. I'll say it. Schmargoyle. Phil Schmargoyle."

"He runs an alley craps game at Bradford and Shittburg."

"Thanks." I turned to leave.

"And Dumpty," said Jake as I paused, "Schmargoyle's an ogre and makes a living scrambling creatures. Don't get scrambled."

"Right," I said.

"And don't get McGillicuddyargoyle killed, either. Don't make me clean you off the wall down there."

I walked away. It was a sharp reminder. Shittburg Avenue was the street The Wall was on. The one where my shining brother Stu met his maker. Nasty business. I talked to people down there when it happened. Nobody saw the king's horses or the king's men. It was all a cover-up. And Jake's admonition was on the money. A treacherous part of a dangerous town.

Don't get scrambled, indeed.

#

When people living near the Org Hotel want to feel better about their neighborhood, they think about Shittburg Avenue. It became the name of the neighborhood, and Shittburg was synonymous with squalor. Every vice known to man. Drug dealers, magic dealers, sex dealers, you-name-it. Literally. There was a guy down there who would make pets that have never existed before. You name it, then you take it home. They call them you-name-its. Totally illegal, but unique creatures are big business. You-name-its were rare, but by and large, if you couldn't find something in Magic City, it didn't exist.

You know what else was rare? A fire-breathing goat.

If you came here in the daytime, it was slightly less disgusting, but we came to see the disgusting bits, so it was around midnight. It hadn't rained for almost a whole day, but that only meant that instead of wet, everything was just coated in its natural slime. The streetlights shone on some scenes and hid others in shadow.

The smells that wafted by were an orchestra of odor; many repulsive, sure, but some to notice were cooking smells. In this urban cesspool, these people knew their simple pleasures. I picked out the aroma of somebody's newt stew, and it was making me hungry.

As I often did as a reflex, I put my hand to the side of my coat to feel that my Glock was still at my hip, where it belonged. The magic in Magic City was tightly controlled, and cops were among those forbidden to use it. Suited me fine. Not that I was above bending the rules for justice, or how I saw it, so yeah, magic came into it now and again. But magic can get out of hand in a hurry, and if you put some authority behind it, everything speeds up. A pistol full of hollowpoints got me through a ton of scrapes, and behaved the same way every single time.

I told McGargoyle to stay sharp and quiet. Just an egg and a harpy, looking for an ogre who knows of a fire-breathing goat. Nothing to see here. Easy enough to stay below anyone's radar, as long as nobody started a commotion.

Street signs didn't last long in that part of town, and weren't replaced, but I recognized when we got to the Bradford Street intersection. All slums here. Three more blocks to The Wall. Not going there tonight, though. Behind the first tenement around the corner on Bradford, I heard noises that you distinctly ignore unless you're looking for a game.

There was a streetlight just outside the alley entrance, so the light shone down the alley. Just outside its reach, deep inside, were other smaller lights moving around, and voices and clinking dice and bones. Gamers.

As I began walking into the alley, my shadow started stretching out in front of me, as a silhouette of my upper coat, collar, and hat. I didn't plan it—and I seldom plan for the dramatic; it's not my style—but when opportunity knocks, I oblige. Anything that intimidates the bad guys. So when the shadow got real big, I stopped. I was about forty feet into the alley, but my shadow stretched at least that far again.

It looked cool, but then McGargoyle came up behind me, and spread her wings.

"Better shadow than an ovoid," she said.

This girl had instincts. And a bright future. And an impressive knowledge of shape identification.

A rumbling voice came from the dark. "That's it for now. Back in thirty." There was shuffling and grumbling, and shadowy figures darting about, some going to some deeper place, some climbing the tenement walls and scurrying away.

A moment passed, and the movement all died down.

"I can come in if you make me," I said.

"No need," said the rumbling voice. "Just as well if they find you in the light. It sends a message."

"Yeah?" I said. "Well, I've got a message."

A thundering thud of footsteps came from the depths of the alley, and a figure slowly emerged into the light. A deep green behemoth, fully Jake's size if not larger. Standing, that meant well taller than McGargoyle, and almost twice my size. Older, too, with cavernous wrinkles gashing a leathery face. Circus fat. Enormous nose and ears, all with ponytails of coarse, black hair growing out. From his head, a broom of ratty, chest-length brown hair that probably couldn't wait to fall out and escape. Dressed in some ridiculous, red muslin tunic thing that could hardly even be called clothing, and a pair of brown sandals.

The ogre stopped about fifteen feet from me. Nothing but concrete between us. Tenement walls twenty feet to our right and left. The street forty feet behind me. McGargoyle had lowered her wings, and she stepped out from behind me and stood at my right side.

"So let's have it," said the ogre. "What's the message?"

"What message?" I said.

"The message you just said you have. Out with it."

"I just said ... wait." I glanced toward McGargoyle. "Did I say I have a message?"

"You did, sir," she said. "I believe it was, 'Well, I've got a message.'"

"That was exactly it," said the ogre. "Word for word."

"Well," I said, "I guess it was actually more of a question."

"You should be more specific," said the ogre. "That was misleading. Thought I was walking out here for a message."

"Sorry," I said. "Unfortunate word choice."

"It happens," said the ogre, putting his gargantuan hands on his hips. "So, what's the question?"

"I was ... that is, we were ... wondering ... wait. Are you Phil?"

"All day," he said. "You got three seconds to get to the point. Unless that was your question. Yeah, I'm Phil. Are we done?"

"Goats," said McGargoyle.

"What?" said the ogre.

"Well, yes, that's right," I said. "Now that the cat's out of that bag, yes. Goats."

Phil swept a mammoth paw toward the blackness. "Does it look like I keep goats?"

"I'm only after one," I said. "And yeah, you'd have this one. It breathes fire."

An actual grin began to form on this monster's cracked, pus-encrusted lips, followed by a smile, then a chuckle, then open laughter I thought was going to bring the slums down on us.

"Ha! You want that one? Haha!"

"Yes, I do," I said.

"Ha! That's rich!" said Phil, still laughing, hands layered over his protruding stomach. "Go find your mother and crawl back in. That's where you belong. Forget about the goat. Haha!"

Phil calmed down some, and when his heaving was over, McGargoyle and I were still standing there.

"All right, now we're done," said Phil. He lowered his hands to his sides. "I'll even let you live. That was a good one. Come back any time you think you can make me laugh like that."

"I need to find the goat," I said.

Phil's tone got sterner. "No, you don't. Run away now. Don't test me."

"He's going to find the goat," said McGargoyle. "You can bet on that."

"Fine. Go find it."

"You know that I need to know what you know," I said. "You know that."

"I know this is where you die," said Phil.

"I don't think so," I said.

Phil held up a little finger. "I could crush you with a pinky, but it's true I'm not as quick as I used to be. Lucky for me, I don't need to crush you."

"Why not?" I said.

He made a chopping motion with his hand. "I've got an icepick spell that'll crack you like an ... egg ..."

"It'll never work, Phil."

Phil put his hands on his hips. "'Phil?'"

"That's your name, isn't it?"

"Well, yeah, but the full name is Phil Schmargoyle. Anyone else in your position would have called me 'Schmargoyle,' and maybe stretched it out a little to imply I should be somehow embarrassed by it."

"You don't find ... your last name ... embarrassing?"

Phil looked at McGargoyle. "You'd have called me 'Schmargoyle,' right?"

"With a hint of perverse pleasure," said McGargoyle.

"Exactly," said Phil. Then back to me, "So ...?"

"So Phil," I said, "your spell will never work."

Phil tossed his hands and looked at McGargoyle.

"He won't say it," said McGargoyle.

"Seriously?" said Phil.

"Fine!" I said. "Schmargoyle! Schmargoyle! Happy?"

"Sure," said Phil, "but mostly because you can't stop an icepick spell."

"Of course I can," I said. "You know I wouldn't come here without magic backup."

"Wrong. You're a cop. You don't use magic."

"Wronger. You know who took down The Caster? Think that happened with just a pistol?"

"Maybe not," said Phil, "but you would've if you could, though, Dumpty. I know you."

"You know diddly."

"Don't change the subject."

"I'm not," I said. "I use magic all the time."

"Right," said Phil. "Ooh, look at me, I'm the cop who uses magic. Dumpty Schmumpty."

I about burst. I wanted to jump around so bad I could taste it, but it was important to stay in my position. But I was bending and waving my arms around to beat the band.

"See!" I said. "See, McGargoyle! That's exactly what I'm talking about! You want to make fun of Dumpty, sure, all you have to do is add 'Schmumpty,' and never mind that that's a detective working burglary, which is another entire thing, but what about 'Schmargoyle?' If you want to make fun of Schmargoyle, what do you say?"

McGargoyle said, "Probably something like, 'You suck, Schmargoyle.'"

"And I've heard that," said Phil.

"I bet."

"Oh, never mind," I said.

"Done," said Phil, raising his arms.

He thought he was going to catch us off guard with the spell, but I'd been watching for that gesture all along.

"Now!" I said to McGargoyle.

The harpy, still immediately to my right, extended her powerful left wing behind me and propelled me forward. I had to tuck a little to get a shoulder down and roll properly, but it felt just like combat school. Between the two of us, my brother Stu was the more gymnastic, for all the good it did him, but I was no slouch.

Meanwhile, Phil was executing his icepick spell, bringing his arms together and slapping his hands, sending the spell wave forward. I didn't use much magic, it's true, but that didn't mean I didn't know anything. I didn't know some things, and didn't know what else I didn't know, but what Phil didn't know I knew was that icepick spells have a convergence point. The wave moves from the caster in two semicircles, meeting at a focal point.

The victim needs to be at that focal point for the spell's strongest piercing effect, and usually the whole thing only takes a split second and the victim has no chance, but I was anticipating. As I rolled forward, the wave went around me. I could feel it, and yeah, the full brunt of that would have been curtains, but it mostly just stung as it passed.

I immediately collided with Phil's huge belly. He was startled, to be sure, because he expected me to be at the other end of his spell, but he wasn't off balance, and he didn't move much. I bounced off and went rolling back toward the street. McGargoyle, though, seized the moment and flew into Phil's face, talons blazing. The ogre took a haphazard swing, but McGargoyle flapped upward out of its path, then swooped again.

I had my feet back beneath me in time to run toward the two while the harpy flapped and clawed, and this time Phil couldn't brace against my impact. He fell onto his back.

He yelled mightily, and flailed a little as he rolled to his stomach so he could stand up again, but as soon as his back was exposed, I leaped onto him and quickly folded my arms around his neck.

"Careful, now," I said. "You're seconds away from going bye-bye."

Phil screamed again, filling the slums with a terrific roar.

"Last one of those, Phil," I said. "Remember, bye-bye."

Phil calmed some beneath me.

"That's better," I said. "Now, about that goat."

#

I burst into Jake's office, McGargoyle right behind me. "You're not going to believe this, Jake."

"I take it you found Schmargoyle," said Jake.

"Did we ever," I said. I stopped behind the right-hand chair facing Jake's desk.

"I have pictures," said McGargoyle, coming up behind the left-hand chair.

First I'd heard of that. "You took pictures?"

"What?" said McGargoyle. "Have you ever seen an egg with an ogre in a choke hold? I hadn't."

"Glad you made it out OK," said Jake. "What did you learn?"

I started pacing in little steps. "It's crazy, Jake. I still don't know if I believe him."

"What?"

I stopped. "A chimaera."

Jake was silent for a moment.

"Well, isn't that unusual," he said. It didn't sound like Jake.

"Are you listening to me?" I said. "A chimaera. You know, lion in the front, serpent in the back, with a frickin' fire-breathing goat head in the middle."

"Right," said Jake. "Yes, that's odd."

"Odd? It's impossible. There was only one."

"Well, so we were told. We may have been misinformed."

"Yeah, Jake," I said, pacing again. "We may have."

"So did Schmargoyle say anything about where it came from?"

"He wouldn't give that up, even as he went unconscious," I said, stopping again behind the chair. "And that's a concern, Jake. Whoever is responsible for it is someone that scares a Shittburg ogre."

"Impressive. Did he say anything else useful?"

"Coupla things," I said. "It's easily agitated and not very friendly."

"Ya think?"

"He said the chimaera likes to play in the big rocks at the west end of Merlin Park. Alone."

"Good to know," said Jake. "Anything else?"

"Make it see pink."

"What?"

"Pink," I said. "I guess it stays calm if it only sees pink."

"At Merlin Park?" said Jake. "How the hell are you gonna do that?"

I started pacing again. "Not sure, but I've got an idea. Right now, I'm more concerned with something else."

"What's that?"

McGargoyle explained. "Flight, sir."

"Flight?" said Jake.

I came to a stop again, as McGargoyle began to walk methodically around the room.

"If this really is a chimaera," she said, "it's only the second one to ever exist, and the first one was only killed by aerial attack."

"Bellerophon on Pegasus," said Jake.

"Right," I said. "We don't exactly have that."

"Not until next week, at least," said Jake.

McGargoyle piped up with a question for Jake. "Detective Dumpty said he was on loan somewhere?"

"Thrumorg," said Jake.

Thrumorg was a smaller city thirty miles away. Magic City often loaned resources to the neighboring towns.

"What's he assigned to over there?" said McGargoyle.

"Murders," said Jake.

"Really?" said McGargoyle.

"Yeah," said Jake, "he's investigating the murders in Thrumorg."

Jake continued slowly as he thought. "So no Bellerophon and no Pegasus. But ... over at the Thirty-third there's a griffin."

"Nope," I said. "Nope nope nope."

Jake chuckled.

"Why not?" said McGargoyle.

"Well, you see," said Jake, "that griffin once tried to use Mr. Dumpty's necktie to build its nest."

"With my neck still inside it," I said. "No way."

"But I had to mention it," said Jake, still smiling.

"So our only aerial capability," I said, "is McGillicuddyargoyle, here, and she's not equipped to best a chimaera. So if we have to go in on the ground, especially over those rocks, we need overwhelming force. We need the Royal Guard."

Jake bolted upright, just like he did earlier, from that itch in his back. "Absolutely not!"

I was surprised by that. I was still standing behind the right-hand chair, and McGargoyle was off to my left a bit. I glanced at her, and I couldn't tell if that surprised her or not, since her expression said she had clearly never heard a gargoyle raise its voice before. I, on the other hand, had endured it countless times.

I couldn't figure out why Jake wouldn't want to use the Royal Guard. It was rare, sure, but far from unprecedented. And in certain situations, standard procedure. This seemed like one of those to me.

"Why not?" I said.

"We can't ... get them involved," said Jake.

There were tiny things Jake was funny about through this whole case, and now this. There was more to the murders at the Org Hotel than either McGargoyle or I had seen yet.

"But that's crazy," I said.

"We can't use them," said Jake, a bit more firmly.

McGargoyle then made a tactical error, the kind that is all too easy around Jake. "But if they spread out, starting at the south end of the park—"

Jake slammed two mammoth fists onto the desk, and the shock wave moved the chair near McGargoyle a little bit. "NO ROYAL GUARD."

There was silence, eventually, and I glanced at McGargoyle, who was frozen stiff, her eyes the size of troll feast plates. Her first lesson.

I knew from way too much experience that we were done there. McGargoyle and I were left to our own devices, and expected to succeed. Against a monster that had only been bested once before, by the son of a sea god and a winged horse that sprang from the severed head of Medusa. All in a day's work in Magic City.

#

Merlin Park was huge. Acres and acres of grass, trees, rocks, sand, with a lake near the center. Areas of picnic facilities, sports fields, hiking trails, all manner of outdoor entertainment. It was very popular, but never felt crowded. To the west of the lake was an area of flat grassland, likely a couple hundred feet across, then a huge arc of natural rocks that were small in front, then larger and larger in crude rows, up to some at least fifty feet tall, forming the west edge of Merlin Park and creating a sort of amphitheater of giant proportions, with the grassland as the stage.

After visiting some loose ends, McGargoyle and I made our way to Merlin Park and traveled east to west through it, wary of when we might encounter the chimaera and wanting to approach it from as far away as possible.

It was a bright day, and breezy, especially around the water. Leaves rustled in the wind, and birds chirped their songs. A pleasing environment, one I witnessed all too little. As we were passing the lake, McGargoyle took off and made a reconnaissance flight further west to see if the chimaera was there. It was.

McGargoyle landed and gave me her report. "It's there! It's on the lower rocks right now. It's big. It's easily the size of that stupid ogre, even without the serpent part."

"Any other people?" I said.

"Not any more, I'm sorry to say. A few burned bodies in some charred areas of the grass, but I couldn't tell what they were."

My worst fear. We didn't reach the monster before it created new victims. We had to get this thing under control, and now.

"All right, then," I said. "Let's work this out before we get over there. You need to fly me over the chimaera, so let's see how this goes."

We were already in an open area, with minimal other potential observers in the park, so McGargoyle extended her wings, and lifted herself above me, facing the same direction.

"OK," I said, "get a good grip on my coat, near the shoulders, and see what you can do."

As directed, the harpy grabbed my coat with her talons and flapped with vigor. Not much was happening, so she flapped harder. I could feel plenty of upward force, but not enough to lift me off my feet yet.

"Give it everything!" I said.

"I am!" said McGargoyle, as she became quite violent with her wings. We did not achieve liftoff. However, to test our buoyancy, I jumped a little, and we did rise several feet off the ground, and took a number of seconds to return. But it was certainly not flight.

McGargoyle released me and collapsed to the ground, panting heavily. "Wow. I haven't … tried something like … that in a long … time."

"You OK?" I said.

She took a few breaths, and was improving. "Yes, fine."

"All right, then, let's try again. Maybe if you grip my coat higher, near the collar."

McGargoyle was recovering nicely, and stood. "It's not a question of where I grip it."

"Weight ratios, then? I'm just too heavy, is that it?"

"For me, yes. But we came close. And that means I might not be able to go up while I'm carrying you, but I might be able to delay how fast we go down."

"What are you getting at?"

"Come with me," she said. We hiked a bit further along the lake, and when we got near the west end, we could already see the grass, rocky backdrop, and chimaera in the distance. When the ogre said it liked to play in these rocks, it wasn't kidding. The huge chimaera was frolicking away with leaps and rolls in the grass, and batting small rocks around. An amazing sight. You hear about these things, but here was an actual chimaera, a beast with a lion's head and body in front, changing to a serpent's body and tail in the back, with the head of a goat sticking out of the middle. And yeah, from time to time, fire coming out of the goat. Damndest thing I ever saw, and that's a pretty good list.

"See how tall the biggest rocks in back are?" said McGargoyle. "Those big rocks in the back are way taller than where the chimaera is, see?"

She was right. "Oh, snap," I said.

"What?"

I reached inside my coat and did some fidgeting. "My left suspender just slipped off my shoulder. Must've moved around when you were lifting me."

"Anyway," said McGargoyle, "if we can somehow get up there and launch, I might be able to keep us airborne long enough to fly over the monster."

"You want us to climb those rocks," I said.

"Yes."

"And jump off, hoping you can keep us alive long enough to make it to that chimaera from above, without getting burned alive or splattered on the low rocks."

"Yes."

"That's insane," I said, walking away.

"Great," said McGargoyle, planting her gnarly wing-hands on her hips. "Where are you going?"

"To the top of those rocks."

#

Climbing big rocks is a tall order for anyone, let alone an egg, but those workouts and gymnastics sessions at the precinct headquarters were paying off. Staying in shape gave me a critical edge against the bad guys; the riff-raff weren't known for their exercise habits. On the slimy streets of Magic City, watching your step had many meanings.

It was more windy up here. Hadn't thought of that. A good breeze was whipping across the grass and up the rocks from the lake. I thought it might help, and so did McGargoyle.

We were on the best launching rock we could find, huge and tall, high above the park. Now we were looking down at the chimaera, who was still thoroughly contented to play in the low rocks and grass. Pulling this trigger was a commitment, because once we took off, we needed to cross at least a hundred feet of progressively smaller rocks, and stay aloft enough to deal with the chimaera. I had a ton of faith in the harpy—her spirit, at least—but this was a tall order.

McGargoyle gently flapped and lifted herself into the air, hovering above me. I reached into my coat pocket and removed our weapon: a tiny swatch of pink cloth, and a small jar of elf spit. Esmerelda was crotchety and obnoxious, and afraid of getting into trouble, but I convinced her that if she was on the city payroll, we had the same boss, and if trouble was her issue, I could get her plenty. Plus, I sweetened the deal with a wad of gargoyle manure, not the most plentiful material in magic circles. Sure, it was evidence in a murder investigation, but there was plenty of it, and I know better than some that fighting crime needs some creative coercion at times. If justice costs a wad of gargoyle manure, so be it; I wasn't going to give a crap about bending the rules.

Esmerelda explained that the magic to turn the tiny cloth swatch into a huge sheet was in her saliva, so when she licked her thumb and pressed it to the brown swatch she had earlier, that made it happen. For the chimaera, the ogre had said, "Make it see pink," so I was betting that I could make a huge, pink sheet of cloth and cover the monster with it. Bit of a trick, but I'd pulled a few tricks out of my shell before.

What to do with the monster after that was an open question, but first things first. If we could get the thing calm, we'd have more time to figure out anything else.

The harpy took hold of my coat. She said it didn't matter where she gripped it, but this time she was higher, near the collar, and it felt more secure. If that somehow meant she could flap her wings even harder without dropping me, that would be surprising, but welcome.

The rock we were on was large enough for me to get a running start as McGargoyle ramped up her flapping, then, near the edge, I jumped.

What was it Jake said to me earlier in the case? Oh, yeah. Don't get scrambled. Words to live by.

We went down faster than either of us were expecting. My butt even scraped the next rock down, but not to injury. The harpy reached back for everything she had, and we moved ahead, still lower but at a much flatter descent.

Halfway down to the chimaera, it saw us.

It reared back on its serpent coil, and the goat head released a massive plume of fire. Just then, the wind off the lake gusted, and the freshly heated blast was enough of a draft for McGargoyle to lift us out of the way of the goat fire.

In its wake, though, we were coming down quickly, but were now nearly above the monster.

"Drop me!" I said.

"What?" said McGargoyle.

I was removing the lid from the jar of elf spit. "You have to distract it. Drop me and fly around it."

"No! You'll be killed!"

"Do it now! Drop me!"

Despite her protests, the harpy knew she had no choice. Brave girl. She released me, and I plummeted directly over the chimaera, but without me to carry, McGargoyle quickly maneuvered to catch the goat head's attention. It blew at her, but she was agile enough in the air to evade.

For my part, I was in freefall over the monster, and I stuck the pink swatch into the open jar and threw it below me.

I heard a faint tinkle of breaking glass as the cloth erupted into a huge sheet. It immediately broke my fall, billowing in huge waves over and around the chimaera. I landed with a thud—but not a crack—on the chimaera's back, at the shoulders of the lion head. I quickly stood at the ready, on the back of the beast, waiting for its next move, but that move was an expected pleasure.

It laid down.

The chimaera came to rest quietly under the pink sheet. Astonishing. That nasty ogre was right about something. Could've knocked me over with a feather. McGargoyle could've, anyway. She had powerful feathers.

I rolled down off the monster's shoulders, and it didn't seem to faze the beast. Its breathing was deep and loud, but calm.

McGargoyle was all smiles as she landed nearby and came jogging over. "Wow! That was amazing!"

"Fitness is important."

"The ogre was right, and the elf magic worked, and here we are!"

"You did good, McGargoyle."

"Thanks! It felt good."

The excitement I could see in her was infectious. Magic City could run anyone into the ground, but when you get a win, when you make life better for people, well, it keeps you going till the next time.

I stood there, facing the pink-covered chimaera, thinking of what's next. "Not bad. Not bad at all. We got this far without getting killed. That was the main thing. But now how do we deal with it?"

"I'll handle that," came a booming voice.

From behind the monster's head strolled an enormous yeti. Taller than the chimaera, but not as large overall. McGargoyle gasped. I shared a moment of shock, but then some puzzle pieces started fitting together.

"Good morning, Mr. Mayor," I said.

The Mayor of Magic City was Pyhole Mealy, as conniving a political animal as there ever was, and combined with his imposing physical stature, a formidable figure.

"And to you, Mr. Dumpty," said Mealy, dressed in immaculately pressed blue slacks, white button shirt, and red tie, as he continued ambling toward us. "This city owes you a considerable debt of gratitude."

"Not to be blunt, sir," I said, "but not much of the city knows about this, and I'm guessing that's by your design."

"You're a passable guesser," said Mealy. "Don't be too hard on Jake. He was under some pressure, and doing his best to follow orders."

"Orders for all this to be as low-key as possible, right?"

"Something like that."

"You got lucky," I said.

"Perhaps," said Mealy, "but I had complete faith that our intrepid Detective Dumpty could successfully put a lid on the situation without undue ... attention. And here you have."

"Here we have," I said, gesturing at McGargoyle, who was nearby to my right.

"Most assuredly," said Mealy, nodding at the harpy. From the look on her face, she had already moved way past any intimidation at meeting the Mayor, and was approaching full irritation that what we just went through was politically manipulated. Welcome to the inner workings of Magic City, McGargoyle.

"I have some other guesses," I said, "but I'd rather hear it from you, Mr. Mayor. So if 'the city' owes us a debt of gratitude, I wouldn't mind if 'the city' could pay it by answering a couple questions. Namely, where did this thing come from, and where is it going?"

"Fair enough," said Mealy. "You've earned that much. And you two knowing this in the future is not the worst thing that could happen."

I glanced at McGargoyle, and it was obvious she read the same message into that as I did. We already knew a big secret, and were about to know more. That could either help or hurt in a given situation, and Mealy was a guy who knew how to make it do either. There was a bit of danger in that, but the kind you can't avoid if you want to make any kind of difference. Pawns don't do much, but you can't win without them, and I was hoping that last part would matter more, down the road.

"This chimaera," said Mealy with a broad gesture toward it, "is a masterpiece of magic. I've always said we have the best of the best in Magic City, and here it sits. Believe it or not, Dumpty, this is a you-name-it. I had it created especially for me."

I wasn't honestly expecting much of a shock from his explanation, but I got one. This monster was far larger than I'd ever heard of for a you-name-it, and it was a known type of creature. Every you-name-it I'd ever seen was a unique, twisted specimen. I was surprised by that, and it must have shown on my face.

"You're surprised by that," said Mealy.

"Not surprising," I said.

"Actually," said McGargoyle, "yes it is. I'm surprised that you're surprised."

"Now that surprises me," I said.

"It took some doing," said Mealy, "and there were earlier attempts that created a variety of … undesirables. But eventually, success."

"So, what, you just needed a pet chimaera?" I said.

The Mayor started strolling out into the open grass, in the direction of the lake. McGargoyle and I joined him. It was a pleasant day, as I was now free to notice, and the grassy area was beautiful. All except for the charred carcasses, several of which were not far away. The chimaera had an earthy odor that was far preferable to most beasts, but the breeze from the lake smelled fresh as we made our way upwind of the monster, who continued relaxing calmly under its pink cloth.

"'Need' is such a strong word," said Mealy, "and less descriptive than 'desire.'"

I was terrible at this kind of conversational jousting. "Also less descriptive than 'illegal.'"

Mealy seemed entertained by my direct approach, rather than annoyed, which was a relief. "Ah, my dear Detective, why are we here but for a little adventure?"

"I can do without the one we just had."

"Regrettable, yes," said Mealy, "but that's the risk that creates the reward."

McGargoyle, who was on my left, with the Mayor to my right as we ambled across the lawn, entered the conversation. "Mr. Mayor?"

"Yes, Officer?"

"That's the where-it-came-from part, but how about where it's going?"

"Ah," I said, "I think I know that part."

"Do you, Detective?" said Mealy.

"The Org Hotel," I said.

"The hotel?" said McGargoyle.

"I had always been assuming," I said, "that the chimaera entered that room through the window and left the same way. But it was already in the building, wasn't it, Mr. Mayor?"

"Very astute of you," said Mealy.

"I'm not entirely sure what a 'stoot' is," I said, "but I take it I'm correct."

"Indeed you are," said Mealy. "There's a reason they don't use the fourth floor."

"I thought it was destroyed," said McGargoyle.

"It was," I said. "Many years ago there was a convention that completely annihilated the place."

"Ogres?" said McGargoyle. "Trolls?"

"Clowns."

"It was vacant," said Mealy, "up until I discovered a you-name-it artist on Shittburg Avenue who could do the impossible. I had the Org fix it back up and paint it pink."

McGargoyle was catching on. "So that's why Esmerelda is on the city payroll instead of the hotel. You needed an insurance policy there, with magic to cover any accidents that might happen, and having a Principal Staff there was unusual but didn't necessarily raise undue suspicions, while nobody knew who was paying her. Nobody who cared, anyway."

Mealy stopped walking. "It's good to be the Mayor."

I stopped and turned to him, and McGargoyle also stopped, behind me. "How long ago was all this?"

"Years," said Mealy.

"And nothing like this ever happened before?"

"Tiny mishaps, but not at this scale," said Mealy. "This time, there were ... circumstances."

"Such as?"

"Ever been married, Dumpty?" said Mealy.

"Can't say as I have." There'd been dames, and some that felt good, but nothing close to a lifelong commitment.

"Then no divorces, either," said Mealy. "Lucky you. Me, not so much."

McGargoyle ambled up to my left side. "You're saying your ex did this?"

"She is … disturbed," said Mealy. "I knew it was a liability for her to know about the chimaera, but there wasn't much I could do."

"Could've dumped the chimaera," I said.

"Trust me, Dumpty," said Mealy, "this was the definitive choice. But when she heard that Bellerophon was loaned out for the murders in Thrumorg, she saw a chance to make life difficult for me."

"She succeeded," said McGargoyle.

"Quite," said Mealy. "So she turned it loose, and when it went down the stairs, the double doors at the end of the hall were open, and that was the way out. But she thought we were left without anyone who could handle a wild chimaera, and she thought wrong. I really do owe you one, Detective, and whatever you may think of me, I make good."

"I believe you, sir," I said. The Mayor struck me as the type who makes sure all debts are eventually paid, in either direction, so I was happy that for now, at least, that scale was tipped my direction. McGargoyle's, too, and a young officer like her could use any goodwill she could get. If she was already on the Mayor's radar, she was starting at the top. Good for her.

"Time to go," said Mealy, turning back toward the chimaera and gesturing that way. "This is good, and really quite resourceful, I must say, but it's not foolproof." He took off walking back to the monster.

I looked at McGargoyle. "You learned some real-world stuff today, Officer, and you handled yourself like a trooper. Glad to have you on the force. You should be proud."

"Thank you, sir. I am, sir. And proud to work with you, sir."

"Can it, McGargoyle. I'm not the Mayor."

She chuckled. "Understood, Detective."

"Now get back to the precinct. I'm a lot slower, and besides, I'm going to hang here at the park for a bit."

"Should I ..."

"Oh, sure, go ahead and brief Jake on all this. It's a happy visit, you'll be fine."

"Thank you, sir." She spread her wings and lifted off. Damndest thing, harpies.

I stood for a minute and watched as Mealy reached the chimaera, still resting under the pink sheet. He stood next to it for a moment, then produced a small vial, opened it, and shook it over the beast. It disappeared into thin air. He either made it invisible or teleported it somewhere, most likely the hotel. Then he shook the same vial over his own head, and vanished. Definitely teleporting.

I wasn't sure if knowing everything the Mayor told us was good or not, but he could have teleported the beast without showing his face, so telling us was his choice, so probably not. But I knew what I knew, and that was that. Just another wrinkle in the fabric of a deeply wrinkled town. The twisted politics and personal games were distasteful, and it bugged me to my core that no one was going to pay for all the dead people. The Mayor was fat and happy, with his pet where he wanted it, and life goes on in Magic City. But at least no one else was being randomly incinerated, and sometimes that's the best you can get.

The lake air was cool and refreshing, and I walked that direction at the kind of leisurely pace I didn't seem to see much. Hell, I didn't even see grass all that often. It was a good day. I'd even heard earlier that the cases in the other two rooms at the Org Hotel had been solved.

That's right. Flumpty solved the rapes in the Room Florg, Schmumpty solved the burglaries in the Room Schmorg, and yeah, I solved the murders in the Room Org.

The name's Dumpty. Frank Dumpty. I'm with MCPD.

END

Bonus Story!!

I really wanted to include this story of mine first published by White Cat Publications online in May 2023, so I'm doing it (I'm the publisher, right?). A western, not a comedy, but something I'm hoping will entertain. Hope you enjoy it!

Morning Sun

Joe Cron

Chet Breen crouched tight against a cluster of waist-high creosote bushes, panting, as he turned to look back through the bushes toward the trail he was just on. Vince Placenko would be appearing at any moment. The trail was the width of a stagecoach, and across it were some larger shrubs and small trees, growing against the face of an eight-foot vertical wall of grey rock. He'd been chased on foot, and hoped his pursuer, not seeing Chet on the trail, would look in the shrubs across the trail as the larger, more inviting hiding place.

In the late-morning brightness, he wouldn't go undiscovered where he was for long. Chet was also noticing that the sun was above the level of the rock face across the trail, and if Placenko did as Chet wanted and looked over there, confronting him in that position might put the sun in a bad spot. He couldn't tell for sure. If so, he'd just have to deal with it. This was the plan now.

It was warm, but not hot. That would come in a few more hours. Chet was comfortable in his dark grey canvas trousers, black boots, and light blue chambray shirt. The shirt was buttoned to the top, with a dark blue bowtie. A grey, wide-brimmed hat, but no handgun or holster. Chet was carrying his rifle when Placenko saw him at the edge of town, and that was still at his side, in his right hand.

Just as well for defending himself. When his rifle was folded in his arms, he was faster than he was with a handgun, which was faster than most other people with a handgun. He kept himself out of the picture for marshal or sheriff, but he knew most folks would want him to be if he agreed.

Chet had too much going on to ever think about working as a lawman. He and his wife ran a small ranch in the area, with two sons and a daughter starting to come into helping age. They were going to be able to grow their operation for years, maybe even generations.

Placenko had a ranch in the area, too. The same area. With one long border right up against Chet's ranch. That was one of the biggest reasons why Chet was being chased that day.

Goats had gone missing from Placenko's ranch. Placenko was furious and blamed it on Chet. That in itself was the result of a series of misunderstandings between them. Placenko got it in his head that Chet wanted to take over Placenko's ranch, so every little thing that came up was seen as Chet trying to run Placenko out.

None of that was true. Chet wanted his ranch to grow, but what that meant for land or anything else beyond what they already had was down the road. As far as Chet was concerned, they could both thrive as neighbors.

Chet had no real clue what could have happened to Placenko's goats, but there was word, days earlier, from a traveling group, that a cougar was sighted in the area recently. Maybe the cat was doing it. Chet suggested as much, but Placenko was having none of it. In fact, after the second goat, Placenko was kind of off his rocker a little. He had no luck getting either the town marshal or the county sheriff involved, so he went after Chet himself.

There was a curve in the trail just before where Chet was now, and plenty of brush on either side. Chet used that to hide when he knew he was out of Placenko's line of sight. He wasn't trying to run away from Placenko completely, just until they were far enough out of town not to endanger bystanders. Then he could confront Placenko and end this stupid thing.

Placenko came into view, running down the path in Chet's direction, gun drawn in his right hand. Placenko fancied himself a tough guy, and was in all black, though he was smaller than Chet, who was nearly six feet. Placenko was darting his head right to left, obviously thinking he would see Chet ahead of him when he rounded the curve. He slowed up, looked around some more for a moment, then took a few quick, cautious steps toward the rock face and larger vegetation across the trail. According to plan so far.

"All right, Breen," said Placenko in a thin, irritating voice. As Chet had heard it, Placenko was born in the U.S., but his father came here from Russia, and learned English, but with an accent that left its mark on the next generation. With Placenko, it was more like just his style than a true accent, but it wasn't really normal. He crept along, taking slow, single steps closer to the trees. His head bobbed up, down, and around as he tried to spot Chet in the brush. "I know you're here somewhere. Come get what you got comin'."

Chet stayed quiet and breathed the warm, dry trail air, filtered through the creosote bushes, so it had that earthy smell like it was about to rain. Creosote bushes did that. He was trying to wait the right amount of time for Placenko to be as far in and as close to the rock as he could be. If he faced Placenko in the open, this could go on forever; better to keep Placenko trapped in one place, even if that made him more volatile.

"Breen," said Placenko.

Something in the tone felt to Chet that Placenko was about to turn, so he stood, his rifle folded in his arms in front of him. "Right here, Placenko."

Placenko spun around and fired a shot. It slashed through the creosote bushes about eight feet away from Chet.

"All right," said Chet without flinching, "I figured on that one. I startled you. But let's talk this out."

"Come out from the bushes and face me like a man."

"Fine," said Chet. Coming out from his hiding spot would let Chet move closer to Placenko, helping both with positioning and aim. Chet began stepping slowly around the edge of the cluster of bushes, keeping his arms folded around his rifle the whole time.

#

Vince watched as Breen walked out from the bushes holding his precious rifle. People liked to say he was pretty good with it, but Vince couldn't believe anyone could sling a gun that large as fast as he could with his Colt. He kept that Colt pointed at Breen for now, low in his right hand, with his elbow bent, but out in front of him, where Breen could see.

Breen kept coming, slowly, and Vince didn't want him too close. "That's far enough," said Vince, when Breen was maybe halfway across the trail, and still maybe forty feet away from Vince. Breen stopped. When he did, Vince slowly lowered his gun to his side, but kept it in his hand.

"You are trying to run me out," said Vince.

"I'm not doing anything of the sort," said Breen. The sun was behind Vince, who was in the shadow of the rock wall, but that was only a couple feet taller than Vince, and the sun was higher and shining on Breen. He was squinting some, and trying to move his head around to use the brim of his hat to shade the sun from his eyes.

"Why do you take my goats?" said Vince.

"I never took your goats. I told you that."

"You are the only one who could. And bits of my goat were on your property."

"Yes," said Breen, "just like an animal would do. I told you there's been a cougar sighting."

"No cougar. Those drifters wouldn't know a cougar if it ripped their arm off. There hasn't been a cougar here in years." As far as Vince knew, it was even before either of them had their ranches there. Breen was clever, and saying that traveling group claimed a sighting was slick. They were gone, so no one could ask them for details.

"Something else, then," said Breen. "Hell, I don't know. Don't know who or what took your goats, but I know who didn't."

"You want my ranch," said Vince. "You said so."

"No, no, no. I've talked about growing my ranch, sure, but so have you, haven't you? How and where that happens doesn't mean taking over your ranch."

"I'm not going anywhere."

"Oh, for God's sake, Vince, if I wanted you gone I could have just picked you off from the bushes, and it would still be self-defense."

"No, you wouldn't take that chance," said Vince. "You're smarter than that."

As Vince was saying that, a shadow moved slowly and smoothly across Breen, and it was obvious he could see much better. Breen quickly unfolded his arms and the rifle swung forward. It was just as Vince suspected; Breen was just biding his time until he could make a move, but Vince was quick. He instinctively raised his Colt and fired, but Breen's rifle discharged just before Vince's gun.

Vince was an excellent shot, but somehow Breen actually had begun to move to his left as he fired. Vince's shot struck him, and Breen spun violently clockwise.

Vince then watched as two bodies plopped to the earth. Breen landed face down in a puff of trail dust. And three feet to Vince's right, the thud of a carcass, with a single bloody gunshot to the head, of a lifeless cougar.

END

About the Author

Joe Cron has been writing professionally for decades, for nearly every imaginable medium: novels, short stories, nonfiction essays, live theatrical productions, radio copy, aerospace technical papers, you-name-it. His current three novels (*Eve of Demons*, *The Holitaph*, and *Alden Bridge*) accompany numerous short stories in the marketplace, in publications such as *Pulphouse Fiction Magazine*, *White Cat Publications*, and anthologies including the *Fiction River* series, as well as independent releases through the Lardin Press publishing house.

Joe is also a long-time musician and singer, with a number of music albums released under his label, Freakish Records. His tracks can be found at most popular music outlets, and most of his work of any kind is available through his website, joecron.com.

Hey, Extra Bonus!

Here's where we find ourselves needing to add four pages of material in order to have the printed version of this be a book large enough for text on the spine, so, for another totally different change of pace, a paranormal romance story! (It adds fourteen pages, not four, but who's counting.)

The White Dress

Joe Cron

The tiny town of Winston Bay lay in the shadow of the redwoods on the northern California coast. Small and hidden, its beauty remained an inadvertent secret from the rest of mankind. Just a patch of sand tucked between bluffs and behind the forest. Less of a town and more like a small collection of tattered grey homes. No stoplight. No post office or businesses. Trees and ocean. Hardly worth giving it a name. A perfect place for a werewolf to stay out of trouble.

One of the local homes had a rickety, three-tiered staircase that led down to the beach, a short, clean strip of sand about thirty feet wide—more at low tide—that ran between the foliage line and the water, behind the abandoned trinket shop that was all but falling down. At the bottom of that staircase, on the edge of the beach, was a rusty, six-foot clothesline pole with a solitary, empty coat hook.

Like the other homes in Winston Bay, the outside was worn, and the grounds, which never included much lawn to begin with, were largely overgrown. But the inside was lovingly well-kept. It was a simple place, with a vintage kitchen, living room, and two small bedrooms, plus a cellar with access through a door at one end of the kitchen. The walls were all beige and the well-traveled, low-pile carpeting was a light green.

In one of the bedrooms lay a worn, sagging, maple fourposter bed. In the bed, on the left side under some tidy blue covers, was Franklin Holt. Franklin was seventy-nine years old, and the rigors of life were catching up. In short, he was about to die. He'd been in and out of hospitals, more in than out lately, but home every few weeks, and now home for the end.

He was not large of stature, five-feet-seven, with a moderate build. His hair was not gone yet, but white and thin, and he had deep, long furrows in his cheeks and forehead. His nose and ears were a bit small, and his lips were narrow, but his cobalt blue eyes were riveting. Not frightening or disturbing, just remarkably intense.

He could see it himself, when he looked a certain way in the mirror. They were wild eyes.

There was a dilapidated wooden chair next to the bed. It was dark brown, but painted so, and there were many nicks and scrapes where the paint was gone. The cross brace between the front legs was fractured, but the two pieces still clung there, the jagged edges now smoother with age and looking almost as if they belonged that way now.

On the bed wall, next to the chair, was a window with frail, thin white curtains. It faced west, so the chair was bathed in late-day sunshine.

In the chair sat Colleen Holt. She was radiant in long, red hair, peridot eyes, and a bewitchingly charming smile. Looking as if she was twenty-five, she was clothed comfortably in a one-piece sundress, white with a small pink flower pattern. She was barefoot.

The sun was low in the cloudless sky, and the moon would soon flood the woods with its signature glow of romance. Mr. and Mrs. Holt languished in a mutually enchanting gaze as Colleen put her hand on Franklin's arm.

Despite the serenity of the moment, Franklin was distraught with the knowledge that the moment was in fact here, and he had never had the emotional integrity to confide in Colleen his deepest secret.

It wouldn't be long now.

#

It was 1956.

The sun was out in all its glory, interrupted only by the occasional puffy cloud drifting by on a remarkable July day. The majestic trees swished in the soothing breeze. The salty Pacific waters were a crystal blue, rolling unhurriedly up to the beach behind the trinket shop in Winston Bay.

Twenty-three-year-old Franklin Holt paused at the top of the three-tiered staircase on the back of his beachfront home, looking over the sand and water. He was dressed only in red swim trunks and sunglasses, carrying a towel and beach chair. He took a big breath of the briny air, savoring every aroma. Fish, seagulls, someone's grilled lunch. Also, at least six kinds of flowers, two different cats, and three or four other animals he wasn't sure about—everything he could detect through a werewolf's nostrils.

Then he bounded down the steps.

He jerked to a stop on the first platform, almost forgetting that the view from there often allowed spotting whales, seals, and the like. The house view did, too, but it wasn't the same as being right outside without glass in between.

Franklin was just about to give up and move on down the steps when he did see a single seal poke its head above water, about a hundred feet out to sea. He waited to see more, because seals usually showed themselves in groups, but this time only the one. Odd. It was a long time since he'd eaten any meat when he turned, and in fact had built his secluded home specifically to help him prevent it, but that didn't keep him from a curious thought about how seal might taste. Seafood wasn't the easiest thing to find in the woods.

Such thoughts were no more than curiosities for him, though. He was committed to a life in which nothing would die during the full moon. His parents were both killed in the attack that left him wounded and cursed, when he was only twelve. They left him a substantial inheritance, but as he was a minor, it went into a trust and he stayed with his grandparents near Mendocino, farther to the south from Winston Bay.

Several years later, it started. Actually, from the time of the attack, his senses and awareness had changed; sight, smells, and tastes all a bit more acute. He also found physical activities easier, with more stamina. For a child on the small side, this was helpful.

Then, at fifteen, the turning started.

The next three years were confusing and terrifyingly difficult. He awoke in bizarre places and circumstances, with vivid memories of the scent, the hunt, and the kill. The things he did—and ate—were viscerally disgusting and yet satisfying an elemental hunger. Between the full moons, everything was normal; during them, nothing was.

He'd heard and read what the normal human media had to say about werewolves, and the depictions were slightly off the mark. In his view, at least, it was in a good way, as movies and such generally portrayed werewolves as being completely oblivious to anything but their instincts when they turned, and that wasn't entirely true.

Franklin wasn't totally vacant during those episodes, and he was aware of some basic concepts such as whether he was about to kill an animal or a human. It was true, however, that the awareness didn't always mean he had control, and so far he had never killed a person, but that was at least partially by chance.

Since he knew he couldn't trust good fortune forever, he took his inheritance at eighteen and built the house in Winston Bay, more remote than Mendocino and with a special cellar designed to help him.

Now standing on the staircase, he was satisfied with himself that for the past five years, he had killed nothing at all, and he fully intended to keep it that way the rest of his life.

He gazelled his way down the steps to the sand, and set up his chair—cloth colored in wide stripes, stretched over a wooden frame, low for sunbathing—and got himself situated for some relaxing time in the warm rays. No one else was around that day, which was common in Winston Bay, so Franklin had the small stretch of sand to himself. Nothing but sun and lapping surf.

He'd been there for fifteen minutes, basking eyes-closed, when a shadow passed over his sunglasses and he heard a peculiar voice.

"G'mornin', sunshine."

He opened his eyes. Standing over him was a small but stunningly beautiful woman with long, red hair and utterly enchanting green eyes. She was naked. She had such an immediate and remarkable influence over him, though, that the nakedness seemed of no consequence.

"I've come a turrible long way," she said. "Might ye help me quench me thirst?"

The voice had a lilt unlike anything Franklin had ever heard. It was familiar—it sounded Irish, in fact—but it was like no Irish accent he'd ever run across. Every word was soothing, enticing, and somehow invigorating all at the same time. Calling it a brogue would have seemed harsh.

He immediately led her up the stairs to find her some refreshment. Inside the house, he scrounged around for some of his clothes she might be able to wear, decidedly without urgency. He came up with some grey sweatpants and a white T-shirt. She was only roughly five-feet-three, so the clothes were large on her but tolerably so. Franklin then got her some water. He had soft drinks, but all she wanted was water.

They had met scant minutes before, yet every moment he spent with her drew him closer and undeniably more attached. There was no explaining any of it—why the oddly comfortable but compelling attraction, why she was on the beach, why she was naked—but he never even felt the need to try to explain it. It was just happening, and it felt quite wonderful.

Her name was Colleen.

Within the next half hour, they were making love. Magical, overwhelming, passionate love. Franklin was utterly enthralled. It seemed to him that Colleen was, too, though there was still no rhyme or reason.

They spent hours together. It was effortlessly comfortable. They played cards, they laughed, they went for a walk, they laughed some more.

They fell in love. In one afternoon, doing nothing noteworthy and everything important, they fell hopelessly in love. The trepidation Franklin always felt about getting close to a woman, with the curse that would be hanging over them forever, was never in his mind that day. There was nothing at all in his mind except Colleen.

As evening approached, Colleen told Franklin she needed to explain something to him. She said she had done things like this many times before, but had never felt such a committed emotional attachment to someone. Franklin was different. Franklin had something special about him.

Franklin indeed had something special about him, and presumed it was the animal magnetism of his condition. Finally, inexplicably, it was doing something right for him, something better, something positive.

Colleen continued with a fantastical story.

She was a selkie, and was indeed from Ireland. Selkies were seals, with the ability to transform into humans by removing their skin. They were enchanting creatures, in the literal sense. She would typically choose a human, remove her seal skin, enchant the human into an evening of passion, then return to the sea that night, usually without the human's knowledge.

It was in a selkie's nature to have these encounters with humans, and by that same nature, they were brief. She had a selkie husband and children. They lived for hundreds of years in those families. It was simply woven into the selkie fabric to periodically spice their experiences by enchanting humans. Her husband did it with human females, and she did it with males.

They never did it at the same time, only separately as the impulse demanded. It only happened every few months, perhaps even longer, and once the itch was scratched, so to speak, the yearning to be back in the sea became quickly overpowering. They would again don their sealskins and return to the ocean until the next time.

What she had never done with a human was fall in love.

Franklin was concerned about her selkie husband, and what this meant for them, and Colleen explained that the selkie families were different. It was a different type of love, a relationship that goes on for hundreds of years, steadfastly but without the passion of humanity. Being truly in love in human form was quite exceptional.

Another part of the built-in emotional barrier between selkies and humans was that once she had been with a man, she could not come in contact with him again for seven years. So even if she might be inclined to be with the same human more than once, seven years was too long to reconnect again. They were predisposed to carry on in an endless series of occasional one-night stands.

She said she had never before explained any of this to a human—there was never an urge to. This time, though, she was so in love with Franklin that she needed to explain herself, explain the situation. It was more than she could hope that they might ever see each other again, but at the very least she did not want him to wonder why she would be gone in the morning.

Franklin felt it, too. There was no question they were immediately and spectacularly bonded. He didn't realize it at the time, but this was without question the single most defining moment of their entire relationship, and Colleen never had a clue.

This was the moment he failed her. This was the moment where he could have told her he was a werewolf.

And he did not.

In hindsight, he found it astonishing that he didn't trust their love. In a single split second, he made a tremendous, terrible choice.

He asked Colleen if their devotion wasn't strong enough for her to simply stay, and she explained that the urge for the sea was just too compelling. It was beyond her control.

There was a way that some selkies remained with humans for longer periods. If a human steals and hides the selkie's skin, they cannot return to the sea. They are trapped as a human, living as human wives and husbands, but always longing for the ocean.

Franklin said he could never imagine doing that to Colleen, subjecting her to a life of imprisonment. Colleen went on to again proclaim her love for Franklin and that she might even choose such a life, but they agreed that it was not worth the resentment she would feel. They could not tarnish what they had, even to be together.

They were both deeply disturbed by their apparent tragedy, but Franklin made a suggestion. He explained that yes, he was young, and it was foolish to dismiss the idea that he might meet and become connected to another human in the next seven years, but the magnificence of his love with Colleen demanded that they at least try. She should come back in seven years.

Colleen said she wanted desperately to believe they could continue their relationship under any circumstances, but was unsure they should make any commitments to a future that uncertain. Franklin said there were no commitments. No risks. She should come back to that beach in seven years, and she wouldn't even have to see him if things had changed. If Franklin was still there and still waiting for her, he would hang a white dress at the bottom of the stairs for her to wear.

She agreed.

With that in place, Franklin rationalized in his head that he would only see Colleen one night every seven years, and that he would probably never have to bother her with the whole full moon situation. At the same time, here he had found the overwhelming love of his life, in a scenario where he would never have to deal with the daily struggles of being a werewolf in an ongoing relationship with a human. He could hold their love in his heart always, and see her once every seven years to rekindle and rejuvenate everything they had. It was absolutely perfect, a blessing he could not have imagined. He was not going to ruin that life by telling Colleen he was a monster, and with that, any possibility that he might yet tell her his secret was gone. Permanently buried.

They made love again and snuggled in for the night in a brand new, maple fourposter bed.

It was impossible for Colleen to sneak out of bed next to a werewolf without waking him, but Franklin intentionally feigned slumber until she was outside. He followed her from a distance, noting that she went straight down the steps to the ocean. She was naked again. She reached between some shrubs at the edge of the sand and removed a black sealskin. She moved down to the water as she began to put the sealskin over her, and very soon thereafter slunk down into the sea and swam away.

Whatever misgivings about believing Colleen's story he may have been clinging to, they washed away in the swirling, green foam. He was in love with a selkie.

He spent that day completely distracted by this monumental event in his life. Not only was he in love, but he needn't be burdened by the complexities of maintaining a werewolf relationship with a normal human any more. This was magnificent!

As evening drew near, he pondered his further amazing luck that Colleen had missed the full moon by a single night. Near dusk, he opened the door at the end of the kitchen and went down the steps to the cellar. There, a thick wooden door with one round hole in it led to a smallish, pink cinder block room with a tattered mattress on the floor. Franklin painted it pink because he had heard of studies that a pink environment had soothing psychological effects. Tomorrow night, it would smell of urine, but Franklin cleaned it between full moons.

Franklin creaked the door open, then stepped inside and pulled it closed. He reached through the hole past his elbow, something that was quite impossible in his turned condition.

Bending his arm allowed him to reach a thick, iron bar attached to the outside of the door, that he could swivel and plant into a hole in the floor, firmly locking the room.

Then he waited until morning.

#

It was 1963.

It was not as bright a day as many in mid-summer, but the overcast was thin and there was no chance of rain. Franklin could smell when there was rain on the way, and today it was not in the air.

It was fairly early in the morning, and the calmness of the weather was in direct contrast to Franklin, who was simply beside himself with anticipation. Now thirty, he was incredibly nervous as the seventh anniversary of the day Colleen left had arrived. The preparations they discussed were all in place. He had installed a metal clothesline pole at the bottom of the beach staircase, with a coat hook on which hung a brand new white sundress with a pattern of tiny pink flowers.

His feelings for Colleen had done nothing if not intensified during the seven years she was gone. He felt possessed by love for her, and could only hope beyond hope that she would remember and keep their promise.

He desperately wanted to be up and pacing, but couldn't bring himself to risk it, as just being on his feet might tempt him to move to the window and look down the stairs, and part of the promise was that she could make her decision without seeing him.

A knock came at the door.

Franklin bolted out of the chair and flung open the door. To his rapturous amazement, there stood Colleen, barefoot in the white sundress. Without a word, they threw themselves to each other and clenched their arms in an embrace that would, that must, last an eternity. They would have held tightly enough to merge themselves together if they could.

They kissed, and cried, and kissed, and embraced again, and laughed at the sheer miracle of being together, and that was all before Franklin even closed the door. Over the following hours, they went on and on doing nothing and everything, as beautifully and effortlessly as if they had just awoken from seven years earlier. The day and everything about it was stupendously magical.

As night approached, they were terrified and thrilled. Terrified that they were going to be apart again so soon, thrilled that they were certain beyond reproach that they would love each other more and more, and see each other every seven years, for the rest of their lives.

It was not a full moon.

#

It was 1970. It was 1977. And 1984, and every seventh year.

It was sunny. It was cloudy. And thunderstorming, and whatever else might have happened on a mid-summer day.

Through the coming decades, every seven years, the white dress would hang at the bottom of the stairs, and Colleen would come out of the sea and up to the house, and she and Franklin would have a day to experience all of the love of seven years.

The year Franklin was forty-four, they got a wild, spontaneous idea and drove to Reno to get married. It took almost the entire day, but it was a wonderfully different kind of adventure for them, and they had a couple hours left in the evening to honeymoon at a hotel in Mendocino.

They spoke from time to time about how Franklin would continue to age while Colleen would not, with her lifespan ten times that of a normal human. It never mattered at all.

And they always went to bed at night together, and the next morning, Colleen would be gone.

And not one of those nights was a full moon.

Until it was 2012.

Now, Franklin lay on his blue-blanketed deathbed, a few short minutes from turning into a monster in front of his amazing, magnificent Colleen.

There was a time when he thought he might simply allow himself to kill her if this were to ever happen. He couldn't stand the thought of her going on after he was dead, trudging through hundreds of years of a passionless selkie marriage, or perhaps even finding another human to share this with. He thought he just might be selfish enough to make sure that didn't happen.

As the sunlight through the thin, white window curtains began to glow orange, Franklin yet could decide to let it end that way.

No. He had to bring his shame to bear and tell her. The only honorable way was to let her life go on, even if it meant his memory slipping into the distant fog.

"Colleen, my incredible love," said Franklin.

"Yes, heart o' mine," Colleen said, that Irish lilt calming Franklin even in this moment.

"I have a terrible, horrible secret I have kept all these many years," said Franklin.

"Franklin, m'dear, if you're meanin' that you're a werewolf, I'm afraid that's old news, love."

"What? What in the world? How could you know that?"

"Ah, the real question is how could I not," she said. "I saw it in those brilliant blue eyes the moment you lifted your sunglasses on that first marvelous day."

This was an astonishing revelation. All this time, she knew. She knew what he was, and she knew he hadn't told her. And it never mattered. Here, at the end, she found yet another incredible way to make him love her more than he could have thought possible.

"Then you know we only have moments left together," said Franklin.

"I do."

Franklin reached under the blankets next to him and produced a large dagger. Colleen nervously straightened up in the chair.

"This knife is made of pure silver," he explained. "At the moment I begin to turn, plunge this into my chest, and I can do you no harm."

He held out the knife.

"No, love," said Colleen, more from instinct than thought.

"You know you have to. I'll kill you if you don't. Take it."

She gazed intently into those wild blue eyes, then silently reached out with her right hand and lifted the knife from his. She held it for a few moments, looking at the blade and turning it back and forth to catch a glint from the final glow of the sun.

"Get ready," said Franklin with some urgency. "You won't have long. Hold it right and get ready."

"There's got to be more time," she said.

"For you and me, there's eternity, my dearest love," said Franklin. "But right now the moon will be up just ahead of the sun, so by the time the sun is gone, I will turn. Quickly, now."

She took the handle and gripped it firmly with the blade pointing out from her little finger, so a vertical stroke would plunge it into Franklin's chest.

"Good, that's—"

Franklin convulsed, and his chest raised from the bed as his back arched in a spasm.

"Now! Now!" he forced out through clenched teeth.

"NO!"

"Ahh! Do it!"

Colleen raised the knife over her head. She stared in startled horror as she saw Franklin's hands begin to quiver and change shape.

"Do it!" he managed to yell once again.

"I'll not kill ye," she said. "And I'll not live without ye. I love you with my life, Franklin Holt."

She swiftly brought the knife down, but deep into her own chest.

"NOO!" Franklin screamed through the pain and convulsion of his transformation.

Colleen slumped down into the chair. Blood spurted and poured out of her chest, soaking the dress red, then slowly trickling down her right arm as it collapsed limply to her side.

Franklin's extremities were longer now, hair multiplying in thick patches. His back spasmed again, harder this time, and he felt a searing pain in his chest as well.

That one was new.

The change was too much. Franklin's heart was too close to the end to survive a transformation. There was one more short seizure, then his body relaxed back onto the bed.

No more convulsions now. No more nights in the cellar. Nothing but the drip, drip, drip of lifeless blood from the hand of his adored.

The luminescent moon crept unerringly into the clear summer sky, gleaming this night on only stillness.

And an empty coat hook on a rusty pole.

END